THE *right* WRONG MAN

AURORA ROSE REYNOLDS

Waking up to a text asking why you stood up your blind date is not the best way to start the day, especially when the man in question is standing half dressed in your kitchen.

Maybe Dakota Newton shouldn't have assumed the gorgeous man with a devastating smile standing outside the coffee shop was her date. She probably— Okay, she definitely shouldn't have slept with him, regardless of how hot the chemistry between them was. But how could she know Mr. Right was actually Mr. Wrong?

Braxton Adams has been called a few things in his life, but a liar was never one of them. That all changes when he's approached by a beautiful woman who thinks he's there to meet her for a date.

As a businessman, Brax knows to trust his gut and never let an opportunity pass him by, so he pretends to be someone he's not.

Maybe he shouldn't have lied. Maybe he should have come clean. But in the end, it doesn't matter, because now he has to prove he's not the wrong man but the right one.

So what if he's not the man she's expecting? She's the one he's been waiting for.

BOOKS BY AURORA ROSE REYNOLDS

The Until Series
Until November
Until Trevor
Until Lilly
Until Nico
Second Chance Holiday

Underground Kings Series
Assumption
Obligation
Distraction
Infatuation

Until Her Series
Until July
Until June
Until Ashlyn
Until Harmony
Until December

Until Him Series
Until Jax
Until Sage
Until Cobi

Shooting Stars Series
Fighting to Breathe
Wide-Open Spaces
One last Wish

Fluke my life series
Running into love
Stumbling into love
Tossed into love
Drawn Into Love

Ruby Falls
Falling Fast

Alpha Law CA ROSE
Justified
Liability
Finders Keepers
One More Time (Coming soon)

How To Catch An Alpha
Catching Him
Baiting Him
Hooking Him

PRAISE FOR AURORA ROSE REYNOLDS

"No other author can bring alpha perfection to each page as phenomenally as Aurora Rose Reynolds can. She's the queen of alphas!"
~Author CC Monroe

"Aurora Rose Reynolds makes you wish book boyfriends weren't just between the pages."
~Jenika Snow *USA Today* Bestselling Author

"Aurora Rose Reynolds writes stories that you lose yourself in. Every single one is literary gold."
~Jordan Marie *USA Today* Bestselling Author

"No one does the BOOM like Aurora Rose Reynolds"
~Author Brynne Asher

"With her yummy alphas and amazing heroines, Aurora Rose Reynolds never fails to bring the BOOM."
~Author Layla Frost

"When Aurora Rose Reynolds lowers the BOOM, there isn't a reader alive that can resist diving headfirst into the explosion she creates."
~Author Sarah O'Rourke

"Aurora Rose Reynolds was my introduction into Alpha men and I haven't looked back!"
~Author KL Donn

"Reynolds is a master at writing stories that suck you in and make you block out the world until you're done."
~Susan Stoker *NYT* Bestselling Author

When Aurora Rose Reynolds has a new story out, it's time for me to drop whatever I'm working on and dive into her world of outrageously alpha heroes and happily ever afters.
~Author Rochelle Paige

Reynolds books are the perfect way to spend a weekend. Lost in her alpha males and endearing heorines.
~Author CP Smith

THE
right
WRONG
MAN

Chapter 1

DAKOTA

"JAMIE, IF YOU'RE not out here in ten minutes, I'm leaving!" I shout down the hall toward my brother's bedroom. I hate waiting. Patience isn't one of my better qualities. And since I know I need to be across Seattle by nine to meet with the leasing office to get the keys for my new place and traffic this time of day is a disaster, my nerves are on edge with annoyance and worry.

"Shut up, Dakota, and pull the stick out of your ass. I told you I was coming and meant it!" Jamie yells back, and I can tell by his tone he's smiling.

I shake my head and glare at his door. Never in my wildest dreams did I think that at twenty-seven I would be living with my little brother in his small one-bedroom apartment. But when I found out my fiancé Troy was cheating on me, I didn't really have much of a choice but to pack up and move from Tacoma to Seattle where Jamie lives.

I met Troy my junior year at the University of Puget Sound, where I was studying broadcast journalism and he was graduating with a master's in political science with plans to work for his father, a well-known politician. The moment we met, I was smitten. He was handsome, well-educated, and he came from a close-knit family, which I appreciated.

At the time we met, finishing school was my top priority, so we took our relationship slowly the first year. By our second year together, we were solid. He was working for his dad, and I graduated and started working for a small local news station, where I was on my way to becoming one of the lead anchors.

"Sis, you're seriously gonna go fucking gray if you keep stressing out the way you do," Jamie says, pulling me out of my thoughts as he walks out of his bedroom followed by a tall blonde who looks barely awake.

"Whatever," I say, biting my thumbnail. I roll my eyes as he opens the door and pats the girl on the ass, sending her on her way like every other woman who has come and gone since I've been living here.

"What?" he asks, turning to face me when the door closes.

"I just don't get why women are okay with spending the night with you, knowing they will never hear from you again."

"I'm charming."

"You're gross."

"What has your panties in a bunch?"

"Like I told you yesterday, I have to be at the leasing office at nine."

"And like I told you, I'll get you there." He ruffles my hair, and I bat his hands away then attempt to kick him, narrowly missing his knee as he moves past me toward the kitchen. He picks up his jacket off one of the stools around the long peninsula that separates his kitchen from his living room.

"You know I hate being late," I growl, running my hands down my hair and smoothing out the pieces he just destroyed, making sure my ponytail is still in place.

"Did you see Amanda?" he asks, and I frown then roll my eyes when I see his shine with amusement. "You can't rush that kind of perfection, sis. It's against the law or some shit." He gives me his roguish grin, the same grin that has women flocking to him. Well, that and the fact that he's six foot two, works out daily, has dark hair and darker eyes, and is the lead singer in one of the most popular, up-and-coming bands in Seattle.

"Can we go now?" I ask, ignoring his comment and waving my hand toward the door.

Shaking his head, he slips on his black leather jacket and tucks his car key into the front pocket of his jeans then pauses, sweeping his eyes over me from head to toe.

"Is that what you're wearing?" he questions, and I look down the length of my body.

"What's wrong with what I'm wearing?"

"That outfit is just—" His nostrils flare and his hand sweeps up and down, signaling everything that's me. "—it's so fucking Troy," he mutters, making me cringe.

Looking down once more, I realize he's right.

Troy always wanted me to cover up.

He wanted me in long-sleeved tops, long pants, and conservative heels.

He wanted my hair up and no makeup.

He wanted me to be the perfect good girl.

And when I was with him, I wanted to give him exactly what he wanted.

"Go change," Jamie growls, and my eyes fly up to meet his.

"What?" I glance at the clock.

"Go change. You don't need to dress like a fucking nun anymore, Dakota."

"I can't be late, Jamie." I stomp my foot.

"You're only going to be late if you don't go change into something else."

"Don't be ridiculous. What I'm wearing is fine."

"I watched you change. I watched my fun-loving, wild sister disappear a little each day over the last five years, but I'm done. I want my sister back," he says with anger and sadness seeping into his tone.

Guilt and disappointment in myself for letting a man change me make it hard to breathe. "I'm sorry."

"Don't be sorry, just go change."

"Jamie," I groan, following him with my eyes as he takes a seat on one of his barstools.

"Hurry. Remember, you don't want to be late." He smiles, pulling out his phone.

"I hate you," I mutter under my breath as I stomp to the suitcase I pushed behind his couch this morning after I got dressed. Opening it up, I dig through, not caring that I'm scattering clothes everywhere as I search for something the "me before Troy" would wear.

Settling on my dark jeans, and a white tank top I normally wear to bed, I find my black ankle booties with a cute heel and carry them all to the bathroom down the hall. Taking off my black button-down shirt, I hang it on the back of the door then pull off the cream belt around my waist. I slip out of my black slacks and flats, only leaving the pearls around my neck as I change into my new outfit. Walking back into the living room, I toss my clothes onto the couch and stomp toward the front door.

"Don't tell me you don't feel like your old self?" Jamie prompts, and I feel his hand wrap around my ponytail. I turn to glare at him over my shoulder as my hair flutters down around me. "Don't look at me like that, and here. You can wear this jacket," he says, holding out a stylish leather coat toward me.

"I'll wear my own jacket," I snap, knowing the leather jacket probably belongs to one of his many one-night stands.

"This *is* your jacket." He grabs my shoulder and turns me to face him. "I got it for you as a goodbye gift."

"A goodbye gift?" I fight my smile as I glare up at him.

"Yeah, I finally get my space back, and you get to say goodbye to Troy."

Tears burn the back of my eyes and I swallow hard.

"I miss my sister, the one who wore a leather jacket every day, the one who would come to my concerts and drink beer while singing along to every song." He smiles softly, holding the jacket out toward me.

Taking the coat from him, I slip it on, noticing I do feel a little more like my old self. Then again, I've been finding me again ever since I moved in here.

"You're kinda awesome," I murmur, stepping toward him and wrapping my arms around his waist.

"What can I say? I *am* awesome." He gives me a gentle squeeze, making me smile.

I tip my head back and look him in the eye. "Thank you for being here for me. For always being here for me," I whisper, and his arms tighten around me.

"I always have your back." He kisses my forehead then lets me go and reaches around to open the door. "Let's go… before you're late."

"Yeah." I sigh, stepping out the door with a tiny flame of excitement in my belly because after today, I will be getting a little of my life back.

I get into Jamie's Escalade that is parked in front of his building and hear my phone beep in my purse.

After finding it, I pull up my messages, expecting to see something from Kathy, the woman who hired me two weeks ago to be an on air host with IMG one of the biggest home shopping television production companies in the US. Instead, I see a message from Troy asking me to call him.

"Who is it?"

Startled, I look over at Jamie, whose eyes are fixed on the phone in my hand.

"Troy, he wants me to call him," I explain as the phone begins to feel heavy in my palm.

"Fuck him. You need to change your number."

"I'm not changing my number." I sigh, hoping he'll drop it. I don't want to talk to Troy, but after spending four years of my life with him, I feel like I owe him something, which is stupid, considering what he did.

If someone would have told me Troy was cheating on me, I would have laughed and told them they were crazy. I thought he loved me. I thought he was going to be the man I spent the rest of my life with. I had no idea that when I was planning a wedding and getting ready to spend the rest of my life with him, he was searching for something else.

"Do you need me to show you the pictures again?" Jamie asks, bringing me out of my thoughts as the city moves by swiftly.

"No." I don't need to see them again; the images are burned into my brain. I still have no idea who sent me the photos of Troy and his colleague together, but I'm thankful to them, grateful I found out the truth about who he is.

Four months ago, I had gone home and checked the mail like I always did, and tucked between bridal magazines and junk mail was a plain envelope with my name scrawled across the front in black permanent marker. No address or any other identifying information, just my name. That envelope sat on the counter for a few hours before I opened it. I had no idea the contents were going to change my life.

Someone had taken multiple pictures of Troy and a woman he worked with in different locations. In some, they were out in public, but most of the pictures were grainy, like they were taken at night, and the two of them were intimately intertwined in the throes of ecstasy.

When I saw the photos, I called Jamie and explained to him what I had received, and even though he may be my *little* brother, he has never acted like it. He showed up an hour later with boxes and all of his bandmates. They packed up everything that was mine and took my two suitcases to Jamie's apartment and everything else to one of their storage units. When Troy came home the next day, I was already gone, but I did leave the pictures along with my engagement ring on the counter for him.

"We're here," Jamie says, giving my leg a pat, and I turn to look out the window, my eyes traveling up… and up. The building with black glossy windows looks intimidating against the backdrop of the dark, cloud-covered Seattle sky. I open my door and follow Jamie out, knowing I wouldn't be able to afford this place if it weren't included as part of my job package.

"So this is where you're going to live?" Jamie asks as the doorman opens the door for us to walk into the building.

"Yeah, crazy, right?" I look around. The lobby is beautiful with sleek lines and modern furniture. It looks like part of a set from a movie. "The CEO of IMG owns this building, where he houses most of the employees, he also owns a building down the block where the offices and the sets for filming are located."

"I'm proud of you, you worked your ass off to get this." He takes hold of my bicep to pull me out of the way of someone walking toward us as I look up at him.

"Thanks," I tell him quietly, looking around a little overwhelmed.

"Don't get that look. This isn't the time or place for tears," he says and I try not to smile, because he really cannot stand when I cry—something I can admit I've done a time or two on purpose to make him see things my way.

"I'm not going to cry." I grab his arm when I see the sign for the leasing office and pull him with me toward it. The automatic doors open for us, and we stop at the desk with a high counter where an older woman is on the phone. She smiles and holds up a finger telling me it will be just a moment, so I smile back.

"How can I help you two?" she asks, looking between us as she puts the phone back in the cradle.

"Hi, I'm Dakota Newton. I'm here to pick up the

keys for my apartment."

"Dakota, I have your envelope in the back. Give me a moment and I'll be right back." She gets up and heads through a doorway. When she comes back a minute later, she's carrying a folder and a large yellow envelope that she places in front of me on the counter, pulling out a few sheets of paper and looking them over. "Okay, so it looks like all the paperwork has been filled out online, so I just need you to sign your lease then I can take you up to your apartment."

I take the pen she holds out to me and scribble my name across the bottom of the document she turns my way. When I'm done, she dumps the contents out of the envelope.

"This—" She hands me three brochures. "—is all the information you'll need for the building. The app to download which will give you access to your apartment so you don't have to use your key card. When the garbage is picked up, the hours laundry service is available, info for the gym and pool, along with how to schedule the use of the freight elevator, which you will need to do when you move in. Now, if you're ready, I'll show you your new home."

"I'm ready when you are," I say, feeling anxious, and she smiles at me.

An hour later, I get into Jamie's SUV with a smile on my face. The furnished studio apartment I was given is beyond amazing and nicer than anything I've ever lived in before. It's even nicer than the apartment I shared with Troy.

Honestly, when Melissa opened the door, I thought it was some kind of fluke, especially with the space being loaded down with high-end furniture. I had no idea the space came furnished, but I can admit I'm relieved I won't have to buy anything except new bedding and linens. She did say that if I wanted to trade out the furniture for some of my own, they would pack it up and move it out for me. It's not needed. Most of the stuff I have in storage is kitchen crap and clothes I will probably never wear.

"So, are you coming to my show tonight?" Jamie asks, pulling me from my thoughts, and I turn to look at him.

"If you promise to talk the guys into helping me move my stuff out of storage on Sunday, no matter how much they drink Saturday night."

"You know they'd do anything for you."

I do know that. I know Jamie's friends have become mine. Actually, they're like honorary brothers who didn't give me much of a choice but to accept them.

"Then yes, I'm coming to the show." I catch him grinning out the corner of my eye. "What?"

"Nothing."

"It's something," I insist, watching him closely.

"You're right. I just haven't seen you this relaxed or excited in a while."

I sigh. "*You're* right. I haven't been." I shift in my seat. "It's just that I finally feel like I'm getting my life back. I have a job and an apartment, and things are finally moving forward again. There was a while there that I didn't know if I would be living with you for the rest of my life."

"You don't like living with me?"

"I like living with you. I can't say I like waking up to use the bathroom and running into your booty calls every night."

"I'm not that bad."

"You're worse." I roll my eyes. "Honestly, I can't wait for you to meet someone and settle down."

"I'm twenty-five. I'll settle down when I'm thirty," he tells me, and I raise a brow. "Okay, forty."

I shake my head. "All I'm saying is you're never going to find the one if you keep looking for the next one-night stand."

"I'm not in the market for a wife, Dakota." His tone softens as he continues. "I know you want that. A family, to get married and have kids, but I don't."

"Never?" I ask, my heart hurting at the idea of him not ever opening himself up to sharing his life with someone.

"I'm not saying I never want to settle down; I'm just saying I don't want that right now. I'm happy with the way things are and just want to focus on my career." He glances over at me with a look in his eyes I can't decipher. "I'm surprised you still believe in the white picket fence after the shit Troy put you through."

"He hurt me, but he didn't kill my dream." I start to chew my nail, but he grabs my wrist to stop me.

"Ever the dreamer."

"Did you really think some guy cheating on me

would change that?" I ask but know in my gut I have doubts about men and relationships that I didn't have before.

"For a while I did, but I guess I shouldn't be surprised that it didn't. Shit, I still remember when we were kids and all the stories you would make up."

I smile at that. "Like when I use to pretend I was psychic and tell other kids their futures?"

"Yeah, and when you would talk for hours about the guy you'd marry, who'd want to adopt ten kids and you'd live in a huge-ass house."

"I still want that." I smile, turning to look out the window, then say softly, "Even if I never find the right guy, I want to adopt. I want to give a child or children a home where they know they're safe and loved."

"I know you do." He presses his knuckle against my cheek where my dimple is, making my smile bigger.

"HOLY SHIT, BITCH. Look at you!" Maggie, the owner of View—one of the most popular clubs in Seattle—shouts as soon as she spots me sitting on the edge of the stage where Jamie and his band are setting up for their show.

When I met Maggie, I wasn't sure what to think of her. On first impression, she comes across as aggressive, with her loud personality and outward appearance. She looks like a rock chick, with her white almost silver hair shaved on the sides and longer on the top in an almost Mohawk, makeup that is always extreme, and outfits that make it look like she walked off the set of a '90s rock video.

"It's just jeans." I hop down to greet her with a hug, and when she lets me go, she grabs my biceps to examine me more closely.

"'Just jeans my ass. You look hot. I don't think I've ever seen you with your hair down or wearing makeup. I'm totally digging the whole vibe you've got going on."

"Thanks." I can't help my smile. She's not the first person who's complimented me over the last few days, which seems a little odd, since I didn't do anything to my appearance but change how I was dressing. Then again, it might not be about my clothing. Since Jamie gave me the jacket I'm wearing, I've felt like I got a little of my power back.

"Anyway, I was going to ask Jamie for your number, but since you're here, I'll just talk to you in person," she says, getting a look in her eyes that puts me on guard. "Don't freak out yet." She takes a hold of my wrist and starts pulling me across the empty dance floor toward the bar. Once we reach it, she plants me on a stool then walks around to the back of the bar, grabbing a bottle of tequila from the top shelf then a salt shaker and a couple slices of lime.

"Are you trying to get me drunk?" I ask as she places a glass before me and pours out a shot.

"Not drunk but pliable." She grins.

"This should be good," I mutter, picking up the shot and shooting it back before shaking my head at the salt she holds out. But I do take a piece of lime and bite into it.

"Now." She pours me another shot, and I raise a brow, wondering exactly what it is she has to tell me. I pray it has nothing to do with Jamie. She motions for me to take the second shot, so I shoot it back. "I have a friend I want you to meet."

"No." I cough, motioning for her to hand me the second piece of lime she's holding.

"Hear me out."

"Maggie." I sigh, dropping my forehead to my hands resting on the top of the bar.

"He's a good guy."

"They're all good guys until they aren't anymore."

"You have a point," she says, and I lift my head to look at her. "I'm not saying you have to date him, but I want you to meet him. Please." She holds her hands in front of her in a prayer position.

"Okay." I sigh.

"Okay?"

"Yeah, okay."

She rubs her hands together, looking far too happy with herself. "This is going to be great. I promise— he's nice, and perfect for you."

"I'll meet him for coffee."

"Dinner."

"Coffee." I hold firm. There is no way I want to sit through an hour-long dinner with someone I don't know and don't like.

"Fine, coffee." She rolls her eyes. "But when you

marry him, I expect to be your maid of honor."

I snort, knowing that's not going to happen. "Fine."

"I'm telling you now; you're going to thank me. You two are perfect for each other."

I doubt that, but still I say, "Tell me about him."

For the next thirty minutes, I listen to her drone on and on about Adam, but if I'm honest, I don't remember half of what she tells me due to the shots of tequila she continues to feed me throughout our conversation.

Chapter 2

DAKOTA

MY FOOT BOUNCES as the cab I'm in fights traffic to get me across town, where I'm meeting my blind date for coffee. After my first week of work, the last thing I want to do is go out, but Maggie called me this morning to confirm I still planned on showing up, and I couldn't tell her no.

"It's just coffee."

"What?" the driver asks, and I shake my head.

"Sorry, just talking to myself." I glance at my phone. Being late, hungry, and exhausted is making me feel more anxious than I would normally be. My first week at IMG was great, but with so much to learn and do, it's taken a toll on my sleep. Then there's getting used to living on my own again. I love having my own space and a bed to sleep in, but I miss having someone around to chat with at the end of the day.

"Fuck." The driver hits the brakes, making me slide forward in my seat, and I place my hand on the glass in front of me to keep from banging my head into it. I sit back in my seat and look through the windshield, noticing two cars have gotten into an accident blocking both lanes. He rolls down his window and sticks his head outside, motioning with his hand. "Stupid idiots, get out of the road."

"Fuck you. Go around!" a large man who looks like he eats small children yells back with a not so nice hand gesture.

"I can't go around. No one can go around!" my driver shouts, pissing the big guy off, and he starts toward the cab I'm in with a vein in his head visibly throbbing.

"I'm just going to walk the rest of the way," I blurt, and my driver turns to look at me. I glance at the meter and take a twenty out of my purse, handing it over to him.

"You're still four blocks away."

"I don't mind walking." I give him a smile and get out of the cab, hurrying to the sidewalk. I pull up a GPS app on my cell and type in the coffee shop then groan inwardly. It's almost a fifteen-minute walk, something that wouldn't be bad if I weren't wearing heels.

With no other choice, I place my purse on my shoulder and move forward, telling myself this is a good way to get in my steps for the day. And I'll have definitely earned the right to eat the double chocolate brownie ice cream I bought a few days ago.

I reach the intersection across from the coffee shop fifteen minutes later and wait for the walk sign with everyone else. That's when I see him. My heart starts to pound, my throat closes up, and my pulse quickens as I take in the imposing figure across the street. I don't think I've ever seen a more beautiful man.

His suit-covered shoulders are broad, his hips lean, and his legs long, thick, and powerful covered in a pair of dark grey slacks that match his suit jacket. The dark-blue dress shirt he's wearing is unbuttoned, showing the thick column of his throat. He jerks his fingers through his hair then checks his watch, his jaw ticking in annoyance, making me wonder if he's mad I'm late.

Someone knocking into me pulls me from my perusal, and I try to pull it together as I move with the crowd across the street. His mint-green eyes lock on me as the crowd around me disperses, and I notice a glimmer of something within their depths that causes goose bumps to rush across my skin like a tidal wave. When he lifts his eyes to mine, I smile nervously, feeling warmth spread down my neck, but then stumble forward when my heel catches on a crack in the pavement. By some miracle, he manages to step forward to catch me with his hand on my hip before I can do a face plant.

"Adam," I breathe as I place my hands lightly on his chest, and he drags his eyes off my lips to meet my gaze. "I'm Dakota." I jerk my hands away from his hard chest and take a step back out of his space, noticing a glimmer of displeasure flash through the green of his eyes like lightening. "Sorry I'm late. Traffic was a little insane then there was an accident and my cab driver was going to get into a fight so I ended up walking," I ramble, waiting for him to say something, anything, and when he doesn't, I start to feel unsure.

Oh, God, what if this man isn't the one I'm supposed to be meeting? I smile nervously, tipping my head to the side and feeling my hair slip over my shoulder. "Please tell me that you're Adam and not some random man I'm accosting on the street."

His eyes roam mine then his lips tip up into a slight smile. "I'm Adam."

Relief fills me and the tension in my muscles eases. "Thank goodness." I swipe my brow and he grins. Good Lord, this man is dangerous. "Mags refused to show me a photo of you. She just told me that you'd be here, dressed for work and wearing a watch."

"That's not a lot of information to go on." The rumble of displeasure in his statement catches me off guard.

"You know Maggie. She's…" I press my lips together then smile and shrug. "She's Maggie."

"Yeah," he agrees, and I wonder why Maggie didn't tell me how intense he is.

"Right." I let out a breath while taking him in then look at the coffee shop briefly, noticing him suddenly get stiff as he looks over the top of my head. "Umm…

I know I said this was just a coffee date, but I'm starving. Do you mind if we go to the pizza place down the block?"

"I have a better idea." He startles me by wrapping his fingers around my upper arm then sliding them down to capture my hand. "I know a great Italian place that's not too far from here."

"Oh." I drop my gaze to our connected hands. I'm sure my palm shouldn't be tingling.

"We'll take my car." His fingers squeeze mine, making my pulse skip a beat.

"Okay." I let him lead me down the sidewalk and almost stumble again when the lights on a Benz flash, and not just any Benz, one of those SUV ones that costs more than I will make in the next two years.

He stops at the passenger side, opening the door for me, and once I'm inside, he slams the door closed then prowls around the hood to get in behind the wheel. Lord in heaven, I don't think a man should look so good in profile.

"Ready?" He turns to look at me as he starts the engine.

"Sure." I take a deep breath, willing my heart to slow down.

"So tell me a little about yourself," he says, looking over his shoulder as he pulls out into traffic.

"Well, I'm sure Maggie told you that I moved to Seattle a few months ago." I shift in my seat and notice his eyes glance briefly at my thighs, making them feel hot.

"Where from?"

"Tacoma." My leg starts to bounce in sync with his fingers tapping on the steering wheel.

"Why Seattle?"

"My brother has always lived here, and he convinced me to stay with him when—" I quickly cut myself off. "I needed a change."

"You and your brother are close."

It's not a question, but I still say "Yeah" as I hold my purse in my lap a little tighter. "Maggie said you grew up here."

"I did." His hands flex on the steering wheel as he presses more firmly on the gas to enter the highway. "How did you and Maggie meet?"

"She knows my brother." I fiddle with the handle of my purse as he takes the next exit. "His band plays at her club every Friday and Saturday." I watch him turn into a hidden driveway and up to the valet parking lane out front of a restaurant named Altura.

"Are they any good?"

"Pardon?" I look at him, finding his eyes on me.

"Your brother's band, are they any good?"

"The best." It's not a lie. They are one of the most popular bands in Seattle, and if things go as planned, they will soon be signed to a record label and sent out on tour.

"I'd like to hear them sometime." He graces me with a smile before opening his door. He leaves the engine running and gets out, walking around the hood. I see him shake his head at the attendant who approaches my side of the car to let me out, and my stomach flips as he opens my door and holds out his hand.

I take it, allowing him to help me down, and then walk at his side into the restaurant. "This place is nice." I look around the dark interior that is decorated in warm browns and golds, with each table seeming private and intimate, lit with only candlelight. "Really nice." I tip my head back to look at him and catch his eyes flash with desire.

"Good evening, do you have a reservation?" the maître d' asks when we reach the podium.

"We don't have a reservation," I whisper, and Adam chuckles before he turns toward the older balding man wearing a suit with a red bowtie.

Recognition fills the man's expression and he clears his throat. "Sorry, Mr. Adams, of course." He dips his chin at Adam—*or is Adam his last name?* Then he smiles at me. "If you'll both follow me."

"You made a reservation for tonight?" I ask as he takes my hand and walks with me through the open room toward a set of stairs that lead to what I'm guessing is the top floor.

"I have a standing reservation." He lifts my hand and kisses my fingers, catching me off guard, and judging by the look on his face, he didn't do it on purpose.

"You have a standing reservation here?" My tone is filled with surprise, because I *am* surprised. Who has a standing reservation at a place like this?

"I like the food here." He shakes his head at the

maître d' before he can pull out my chair for me and comes around to stand behind me to do it himself.

I take the seat when he nods for me to do so then accept a menu. I hold it up, nibbling my bottom lip and trying to figure out who this guy is. I know I was a little drunk as I listened to Maggie tell me about him, but I feel like I would remember her saying he's loaded. Okay, I don't know that he's loaded, but judging by his ride and the cost of an appetizer at this place, I'm going to assume he is. Then there's the fact that the maître d' addressed him as Mr. Adams, meaning Adam is his last name not first. Why would Maggie tell me his name is Adam?

"Is Adam your last name?" I blurt the question, looking at him over the edge of the menu.

"It is." I study him as he places a napkin on his lap.

"So what's your first name?"

"Braxton." Interesting, that name fits him better, but it still doesn't make sense. "A lot of people call me Adam, Maggie being one of them."

Okay, I guess that makes sense. "And you're in banking?" I remember Maggie telling me that, or I'm pretty sure I remember her saying something about it.

He leans forward, not answering my question, placing his elbows on the table. "Are you okay?"

"Yeah." I lick my lips then glance around, feeling like being in his presence and in a restaurant this nice is too much for me to handle.

"What's wrong?"

I focus on him, and before I can think, the truth

spills out. "It's just, Maggie told me that you were handsome, but she didn't prepare me fully, and then your car, and this place…" I wave my hand around. "I feel like I should have had a little more warning about you."

"You don't like my car?" He sits back, raising a brow.

"I'm not saying that." I shake my head. "I just know it's expensive, and everything on the menu here is more than I spend on groceries in a week." I look around the empty space and wonder if this is where he always sits when he's here, away from everyone else. This seems like somewhere a CEO would bring potential clients, not somewhere a guy just wanting a warm meal would sit.

He reaches for my hand, gaining my attention, and I notice his expression has softened. "How do you feel about cheap Chinese food?"

"Would you think less of me if I told you I love it?"

"No."

"Then I love it." I sigh, placing my menu down.

"Let's go." He stands, tossing the napkin from his lap onto the table, and my brows draw together.

"Where are we going?" I ask, wrapping my fingers around his as he pulls me up to stand.

"To eat Chinese."

I blink at him in disbelief, but he just ignores me and leads me back down the stairs through the restaurant and out the door, where his car is still waiting to be parked. He opens the door for me to get in, and then a moment later, he gets in behind the wheel.

"I didn't mean we had to leave," I say, turning in my seat toward him.

"I know." He starts the engine then grabs his phone, typing something in. Seconds later, the sound of a phone ringing fills the silence. "What do you want to eat?"

"You're serious?"

"I'm always serious."

I believe that. I really, really believe that.

"Gorgeous, are you going to stare at me or tell me what you want to eat?" he asks as a distinctively Asian voice comes through the car speakers.

"Chicken lo mien," I say softly then listen to him place his order and mine before ending the call.

"Are they going to be mad you left without saying anything?" I ask as he puts the engine in drive and pulls away from valet.

"I don't care if they are." He stops at a red light, and I feel his eyes on me as I chew my lip, trying to process everything that's happened. "What are you thinking about?"

"Maggie didn't tell me how intimidating you can be."

"I intimidate you?"

I want to laugh. I bet he intimidates everyone he meets. "You're a little overwhelming."

"Overwhelming?" he repeats, sounding like he doesn't understand.

I try again. "You seem like you're a lot to handle."

"What makes you say that?"

"I don't know." I lick my lips. "I'm still trying to figure it out."

"Let me know when you do." He winks and my stomach flutters.

We drive the rest of the way to the Chinese restaurant in silence, and when we arrive, he double parks and gets out, holding the door open and locking eyes with me. "I'll be right back."

"I'll be here," I say, and he slams the door. I watch him go into the restaurant and notice there's a long line. I start to pull my phone out of my bag, but red-and-blue lights flash and I turn to look over my shoulder. "Shit." I unhook my belt and fall across the middle console. Just as I'm seated behind the wheel, there's a tap on the window. It takes me a moment to find the button to roll it down, and when I do, the officer standing on the other side of the door shakes his head.

"Ma'am, you can't park here."

"I'll just be a minute. My… um… friend went in to pick up our food." I glance quickly at the restaurant and see Braxton's head a foot above everyone else's, still waiting to reach the counter.

"Sorry, you gotta move."

"But—"

"Move or I'll give you a ticket."

"Okay," I give in, and he jerks up his chin then heads back to his car.

My heart starts to pound as I watch him get into his vehicle and know when he doesn't pull off that he's waiting for me to leave. With no other choice, I adjust the seat so I can actually touch the pedals then put the engine in Drive. I hold my breath as I flip on the turn signal and wait until it's clear to pull into traffic. I turn right at the next stop sign then curse when I see that the next road is blocked off, sending me deeper into an area that doesn't exactly look welcoming.

When I'm finally able to go right again, I do then drive like an old lady until I reach the road the restaurant is located on and turn once more. When I see the bright yellow awning for Number 1 Chinese, I notice the cop is still in his cruiser but pull in to park when I spot Braxton at the counter. I'm just about to hop back over to the passenger seat but stop when the cop flashes his lights at me, signaling for me to move along.

Damn.

With a few unladylike curses, I head down the block once more, knowing Braxton is going to assume I jacked his car and I have no way to let him know I didn't and am actually just doing him a favor. When I make it back around once more, I see Braxton standing on the edge of the sidewalk with a bag of Chinese food in one hand, looking at his cell in the other.

I honk and he lifts his head as I roll down the passenger side window. "A cop told me I had to move it or he would give you a ticket."

"I thought you stole my car." He steps off the ledge of the sidewalk into the road and opens the door, getting in and slamming it closed.

My eyes widen. "Don't you want to drive?"

"I'm gonna have to double park again in about two minutes. It's better if you stay where you are," he says, buckling up.

"I don't think that's smart. I almost had a heart attack driving around the block two times."

"I trust you."

"You trust me, but you thought I stole your car." I shake my head. "That doesn't really make much sense."

"You didn't steal it. You moved it so I wouldn't get a ticket."

"I'm starting to think you're a little insane." I hold up two fingers an inch apart.

His eyes move to my fingers and he grins. "Maybe. But isn't everyone a little crazy?"

"Maybe," I agree then ask, "Where am I driving us?"

"The corner store at the end of the next block."

Right. I pull back out into traffic and drive us there then watch as he gets out, only to come back a minute later with a brown paper bag. He comes around to the driver's side and opens the door, reaching across me to unhook my belt.

"I'll take it from here."

Thank God, I think but don't say. Still, he must read my expression, because he chuckles as he helps me down only to walk me around to the passenger door and help me in. "Where are we going?" I ask once I'm buckled in and he's pulling away from the curb.

"Freeway Park, it's not far from here."

"Well that screams horror movie," I mutter under my breath then inwardly smile at the sound of his laughter. When we reach the park, he pulls into a spot on the street and gets out, going to the back door to grab the stuff he picked up.

I meet him on the sidewalk and marvel at the ease I feel as he takes my hand, carrying the bag of our food in the other.

"Have you been here before?"

"No, but it's beautiful." I know my voice is filled with awe as I look around. With the sun just starting to set and the buildings all lit up, it looks like a postcard.

"Just wait until I show you the labyrinth." He leads me down a tree-lined path to a large fountain surrounded by curved benches then motions for me to take a seat.

I sit and watch him unload our food from the bag then trade out my fork for a set of chopsticks before opening up my paper container. Starving, I dig into my noodles with abandon, not caring how I look shoving them into my mouth.

"Thank you for this," I say as he takes a seat next to me and opens his container.

"For what?" he asks, and I fiddle with my chopsticks.

"It's been a long week." I shake my head. "I needed this, a simple meal in a quiet place."

"What happened this week?" he asks before taking a bite of his noodles.

"I started a new job." I turn toward him. "I worked

at a small news station before I moved here, but I just started working for IMG, and I feel a little out of my league." I notice his eyes flare slightly but don't ask what that's about. "There have just been a lot of changes for me in the last week, and I guess I'm still trying to settle in."

"Do you like your new job?"

"Yeah, it's a lot more intense than I'm used to, but I like my boss and the team I'm working with. Everyone seems really nice. It's just different."

"Sometimes different is good," he says softly, and I have to agree with that. "With time, you'll settle in and find your footing. They wouldn't have hired you if you didn't have what they were looking for."

"You're right," I agree. Kathy, my boss, told me something along the same lines today after my first time on air.

"I'm always right." He winks, and I can't help but laugh. He watches me for a moment then shakes his head and sets his food aside. He picks up the paper bag he came out of the corner store with and pulls out a cardboard container and two red solo cups. "Keeping with the theme." He hands me a cup. "Wine from a box."

Laughing once more, I hold out my cup for him to pour me a drink. "You know the way to my heart."

"I'm not upset you're so easy to please."

"I like cheap food and wine, but I'm definitely not easy," I say in all seriousness.

"Noted." He lifts his cup and I do the same. "Here's

to positive changes and settling in."

"I'll toast to that." I touch my cup to his then take a sip, trying not to show exactly how gross it is.

"Wow, that tastes like I bought it from the corner store for four dollars," he says, wiping his mouth with the back of his hand, and I laugh. God, when was the last time I laughed this much with a man who wasn't Jamie?

"It's not so bad." I attempt to take another sip but end up gagging when the smell hits my nose.

"It's worse?" He stands, taking my cup from me. "I'll get you a glass of real wine when we leave here," he promises and walks both cups and what's left of the box to the trash. When he comes back, he nudges his knee against mine. "Eat up so I can show you the labyrinth and get you a drink."

"Is there any chance that when you say you're going to show me the labyrinth, you're referring to the movie and actually mean you're taking me to meet Jareth and Hoggle?"

His eyes flash with approval. "I don't want to crush your dream, but unfortunately, David Bowie and that grumpy puppet won't be around."

"Darn, and here I was starting to think this might be a night to remember."

"The night's still young," he rumbles, and I press my thighs together when I see a look of promise in his gaze.

Lord, I'm in so much trouble.

Chapter 3

AFTER SHOWING ME the labyrinth, a cool area of the park with staircases going in all different directions we got back into his Benz and ended up at a small bar near my building, our table tucked into the window alcove away from everyone else.

"Favorite food?" he asks, leaning closer to me, my knees trapped between his powerful thighs as his body almost cages me in, making everything around us disappear.

For the last forty minutes or so, we've been playing this game, but even though the questions are completely innocent, they seem to be amplifying the undercurrent of sexual tension building by the minute.

"Tacos," I answer before taking a sip of wine.

"Steak."

"Red meat—not surprising." I smirk as his lips twitch.

"Favorite song?" he asks.

"'Hello' by Adele. You?"

"'Runaway Train.'"

"Really?" I eye him doubtfully and he grins.

"Really. Now, favorite color."

"Purple."

"Not pink?"

"No." I make a face.

I listen to him chuckle then watch his lips move as he speaks. "Black for me."

"Again, not surprising."

"It's not?" He lifts his glass of amber liquor to his lips.

"Not at all. Black is a dominant color, and that seems to be your thing."

"Dominance is my thing?" He raises one sharp brow.

"Isn't it?"

"I don't know. I've never put a label on myself before or had anyone else attempt to dissect me." He sits back then eyes my almost empty glass briefly. "Do you want another?"

"Yes please." I smile, and he skillfully moves my legs from between his to stand.

I hold my breath as he bends, skimming his nose along my cheek, and then I close my eyes as he whispers, "Be right back."

"I'll be here," I say breathlessly, catching the small

smirk on his lips as he leans back. I watch him move across the bar, noting I'm not the only woman admiring all that is him. I pick up my glass and turn toward the window that looks out over the street and smile as a couple passes, holding hands with a little boy between them who's attempting to do a backflip.

"Is this seat taken?" I look over my shoulder and come face-to-face with a man standing way too close.

"Umm." Before I can say more, he pulls out Braxton's chair and sits, setting his beer down on the table. "Sorry." I try not to sound annoyed, even though I am. "I'm here with someone."

"Really?" He looks around. "Where are they?"

"At the bar," I say, and he looks toward the bar, and I follow his gaze but don't see Braxton anywhere in sight.

"I'm sure your friend won't mind if I keep you company." His arrogance is not as charming as he thinks it is, and I feel tension start to settle in my neck and shoulders. "So what's a pretty girl like you doing here on a Friday?"

A pretty girl like you? Really? I fight the urge to roll my eyes. "As I mentioned after you sat down, I'm here with someone. They should be back any minute."

"Right." He smiles like he doesn't believe me and picks up his beer. "So do you live around here?"

"Why?" I ask and move away when he tries to cage me in like Braxton had me minutes ago.

"Just making small talk. I live in the building across the street." Shit, does that mean we live in the same building? "What about you?"

"I'm new to the area," I answer vaguely, and he thumbs the label that's beginning to peel off his beer.

"I'd be happy to show you around sometime."

Lord help me. "I—"

"Sorry it took me so long, baby." Braxton appears out of nowhere, cutting me off, setting a glass of wine next to my now empty one, and cupping the back of my neck with his hand before turning to look at the man in his seat. "Thanks for keeping my girl company."

Whatever his name is—his eyes widen like he's just seen a ghost and he practically falls out of the chair. "Shit, sorry, so sorry," he rushes out then stumbles away from the table. I watch him rush across the room, wondering why he looks like his life just ended.

"Are you all right?" Braxton asks, stealing my attention by moving his hand around to cup my cheek, and my eyes lock with his.

"Yeah."

He searches my gaze for a long moment before taking his seat, caging me in once more, and just like that, the buzz that runs across my skin in his presence is amplified. I pick up my new glass of wine and take a gulp then set it down, wondering if I should do what I want to do.

"What are you thinking about?"

Asking you back to my place. Before I can make something up, people start shouting, and we both look toward the bar where a fight is breaking out.

"Fuck, let's get out of here," he says when a

barstool is thrown across the room. Without giving me much of a choice, he stands and pulls me up with him. Then before I even know it, we're standing outside. He takes off his suit jacket and swings it around my shoulders, helping me into it before he starts down the sidewalk, holding my hand.

Then, just like it's prone to do in Seattle, the skies open up and rain begins to fall. Not a little but a lot.

Thinking, *Screw it,* I throw caution to the wind and pull him under an awning by tugging on his hand. "I live just down the street," I shout over the pounding rain and nod toward my building that can be seen over the others on the street. "We could go there and dry off."

I can't understand the look in his eyes but let out the breath I was holding when he squeezes my fingers. "Lead the way."

I don't lead him. Then again, I doubt anyone has ever led him in his life. He pulls me across the street when the traffic is clear, and by the time we make it to the entrance of my building, we're both soaking wet. I acknowledge the doorman with a small smile then head for the elevators.

I laugh when I catch my soaked reflection in a mirror on the wall then look up at him when he joins in. I press the button, and when the doors open, we fall inside still laughing. I hit the number for my floor, and as the elevator rises, I shiver from being wet in the air conditioning.

"Come here." He drags me against his chest, and I

soak in his warmth and scent until the doors open once more. We step out of the elevator and walk down the hall, and when we reach my door, I pull my phone out of my purse and tap it to my keypad and let us in. I flip on the lights and take off his jacket, hanging it on the handle, and then move to the kitchen.

"Do you want some tea or something?" I ask, and his eyes pull away from my place and focus on me. "I might have some Jack from when my brother and his bandmates helped me move in."

"I'm good with water." He follows me, and I fill up a teakettle, placing it on the stovetop before grabbing a glass for him and filling it from the tap. I hand it to him then go in search of towels. "Your place is nice."

"Thanks." I look around. I got a few purple pillows to add some color to the black couch and a silver-and-white throw that matches my bedding but haven't done much else. "It was furnished when I got it, so I can't take credit for the furniture."

"Hmm." He walks to the wall of windows and looks out over the city as I go to my bathroom. I take off my dress and undergarments and change into a pair of leggings and a tank then grab two towels and walk to where he's standing, handing him one while using mine to dry my hair. "I don't have any clothes that will fit you, but I can toss your shirt in the dryer if you want."

"That'd be good." He unhooks his cufflinks then pulls the bottom of his shirt from his pants before working on the buttons. I try not to stare at him, but it's impossible not to admire his fingers as they work or his torso as he bares it to me.

Once his shirt is off, I take it from him with my shaking hands. I don't look at him as I walk across the room to the dryer to toss it in. As I press start, the teakettle whistles, so I go to the kitchen, grab a peppermint teabag, fill my cup with steaming water, and carry it to the couch. As soon as I'm seated, he joins me, so I hand him the throw.

"Is this because you think I'm cold or because you're trying to cover me up?"

"Both," I admit, and he places the blanket over his lap, leaving his chest visible, and I shake my head then look over the back of the couch. "It's still raining."

"It's supposed to rain most of the night." I feel his fingers skim my cheek then turn to watch him twirl a piece of my hair around his fingers. "It's one of the things I love about this city."

"Most people from here hate the fact that it rains all the time."

"Like you've pointed out, I'm not like most people." He trails his finger around the shell of my ear, and then his hand slides into my hair so he can cup the back of my head and pull me closer. His breath whispers into the quiet, and my eyes slide closed as his lips press against mine. His thumb on my chin gives a silent demand to open for him, and I do, moaning when his tongue touches mine. When he pulls away, I start to ask him why he's stopping, but my breath catches as he flips away the blanket and pulls me over to straddle his lap. "That's better."

He smiles before dragging my mouth back down to his. I have to agree; this position is much better. I move my hands up his chest and wrap them around his shoulders as his hands glide up the tops of my thighs then around my hips, urging me closer.

I get completely lost in him, his touch, his kiss, his taste, and don't care if I'm never found as his mouth trails down my neck to the tops of my breasts.

"Lift your arms."

I don't hesitate. I lift my arms up over my head, and he lifts my tank over my stomach then breasts, eventually tossing it away. My nipples pebble under his gaze, and I hold my breath as he takes me in.

"Perfect. Absolutely perfect." He cups both my breasts then dips his head, taking one hard peak between his lips. I whimper, sliding my fingers through his hair, then groan in frustration when he captures both my wrists, pulling them behind my back and leaving me completely at his mercy as he devastates me with his mouth.

Panting for breath, I call out his name, and he stops to look at me. His eyes are so dark with desire that I know he's feeling just as desperate as I am. I try to tug my hands free from his hold, but his grip just tightens.

"Dakota…"

"Braxton." My chest rises and falls rapidly as he stands and walks across the room, carrying me with him.

The moment my back hits the bed, he comes down

on top of me, kissing me deeply before pulling back to look at me. "Keep your hands above your head."

My inner walls tighten at the command, and I lift my hands above me and watch him lean back then stand. I see him kick off his shoes then remove his belt and pants before leaning over me, kissing my stomach. He grasps my leggings at the waist to pull them down my thighs.

I'm not ready for his mouth as he spreads my legs and buries his face between my thighs. It kills me to keep my hands where they are, but I do, and he rewards me for my efforts by sliding two fingers inside me and using them against my G-spot. My thighs shake as he sucks on my clit, and then my mind blanks as I fall over the edge into blinding white light that licks across every inch of my skin. I come back to myself as he kisses my inner thigh then my stomach and breast.

When he reaches my mouth, he smooths my hair back away from my face, and I watch him smile. "You listened."

"I did." I wrap my legs around his waist then move my hands to his biceps as his hand glides up my side, making my skin tingle. "I'm a very good girl."

"I think I should test that." He kisses me before rolling us so that I'm straddling his hips, and feeling all that is him between my legs, I swallow hard. "Tell me you want this, Dakota."

I look into his eyes and know without a shadow of a doubt I want this. I want him. "I want you."

The moment those three words leave my mouth, he

leans up to kiss me. Then for the rest of the night, we get lost in each other.

———————————

THE SMELL OF coffee seeps into my unconscious mind, pulling me from sleep. I slowly blink my eyes open, seeing nothing but the edge of my pillow and the empty expanse of my bed. I shift from my stomach to my side and bite back a whimper. I feel like I've been branded from the inside out, and every muscle in my body feels deliciously used.

Braxton.

I lift my head slightly off my pillow and scan the open room of my studio, in search of the man responsible for making me feel the way I do right now. When I find him in my kitchen, I hold my breath as I study him, wanting a moment to take him in before he realizes I'm awake.

Even leaning casually, with his back to the counter, one hand with his long fingers curved around his bare hip and the other holding his cell to his ear, he looks like he owns the place. I can't hear what he's saying, but his lips are moving quickly as he speaks, and from his expression, it seems serious. Despite his intensity, Maggie was right; he's perfect—maybe even perfect for me.

I can't remember a time when I've felt so at ease around a man. Even when Troy and I first got together, I was on edge, waiting to do or say something that didn't go along with his plan and would piss him off.

There was always a silent demand for me to act a certain way, because of his job and his father's position.

Last night with Braxton, I felt like I could be myself, like he wanted me to be exactly who I am. It was refreshing and freeing, and if I'm honest, he made me feel like I'm good enough.

"Gorgeous, are you going to stare at me or are you going to come give me a kiss and get a cup of coffee?"

I blink at those words and focus on him, watching his lips tip up into a roguish grin.

"Umm…" I bite my lower lip then let it go to mutter, "I could use some coffee."

"Then come here." He motions me forward with one finger, and I know that if he was any other man, I might not think that was hot. But coming from him, I feel my body respond.

I toss back the covers, and cool air hitting every inch of my skin makes me freeze in place. I quickly pull the blankets back over me and swear I hear him chuckle. I don't even look at him as I search the bed and floor for something to cover myself with. Not seeing anything within reach, I decide the sheet will have to do. I tug it with a grunt from the end of the bed and wrap it around me before pushing the covers back once more.

I blow a piece of my hair out of my face when I stand then look at him, catching him smiling. "I'll be right back."

"I'll be here." He lifts his cup of coffee toward me and winks.

I give him a nervous smile then look down at my cell phone when it lights up with an incoming message. I pick it up, taking it with me to my bathroom, and quickly put on a robe and brush my teeth. When I'm done, I look at my phone and notice I've got a few messages and missed calls—something that isn't normal.

The first text I open is from Maggie asking why I stood up Adam. The messages to follow are from Jamie asking if I'm okay. I shake my head in confusion and text both of them back, letting Maggie know I did meet up with Adam, and telling Jamie I'm at home and fine. Before I even have a chance to set my cell down, Maggie messages back in all caps.

MAGS: HE WAS SITTING ON A STOOL AT MY BAR ALL NIGHT, SO YOU DIDN'T MEET WITH HIM.

I glance at the bathroom door as a heavy weight starts to fill the pit of my stomach. If Adam was at View all night, who the hell is the man in my kitchen right now?

I text back as quickly as I can with my hands shaking.

ME: ARE YOU SURE?

MAGS: AM I SURE? YEAH, I'M SURE. HE WAS WAITING FOR YOU AND YOU NEVER SHOWED UP, SO HE CAME TO THE CLUB.

"Oh my God," I whisper, feeling sick.

I couldn't be wrong about the man I willingly gave myself to last night, could I? What the hell was I thinking? I didn't really ask questions. I let him lead the way, charmed by his good looks and dominance. My throat gets tight as anger fills me from the tips of my toes to the roots of my hair.

Without thinking, I grab the knob and pull the door open. I storm past my bed toward my kitchen, willing my feet to hold steady as I move with purpose toward the man watching me.

"Morning, beautiful."

My throat gets tight remembering how I got off to him calling me that last night.

"Who are you?" I ask, shoving my hand against his shoulder with enough force that the cup filled with coffee he's holding sloshes out over his hand and onto the floor.

"What?" His confused expression angers me more.

"Who are you? I know you're not the guy I was supposed to meet!" I yell, and I see it then, a look I witnessed from him numerous times last night but didn't dissect. A look of anxiousness, maybe even fear of being found out. God, how stupid am I?

"Dakota—" He takes a step in my direction, and I hold up my hand palm out, not trusting myself to handle the pull I feel when it comes to him.

"Just tell me the truth." My hands ball into fists at my sides, and he sets the cup on the counter then leans back against it like he doesn't have a care in the world.

"The moment I saw you, I wanted you."

My eyes narrow on his. "The moment you saw me, you wanted me, so you pretended to be someone you're not?"

"Yeah."

Yeah? Just yeah?

"I can't believe this." I rub my hands down my face, wondering how I ended up in this situation.

"Baby."

"Don't call me that," I hiss, dropping my hands away to glare at him. "I don't even know you."

"You know me," he counters, glancing at the bed before looking me in the eye. "We definitely know each other."

"I thought I knew you." I shake my head in an attempt to keep the disappointment I'm feeling from showing. "All I know now is you're a liar and I'm an idiot."

"You're not an idiot."

"Oh yeah, I am. I should have—" I wave my hand out, cutting myself off before I can tell him that I should have known he was too good to be true. "You need to leave."

"We should talk." He takes another step toward me, and I back up before he can touch me, catching pain flash through his eyes. But I tell myself it's just my imagination. "Dakota—"

"Please." My eyes slide closed. "Please just leave." I know I sound desperate. I feel desperate for this to be over, for him to be gone so I can forget last night, forget what I thought I felt and what we shared.

"If I leave now, I want you to understand this isn't over." There's no ignoring the threat in his statement. I focus on him, really focus on him, noticing his demeanor may seem relaxed, but his muscles are bunched like he's just waiting for the right moment to strike. "We're not over."

"There is no we. I don't even know who you are."

"You will."

I swallow then take a step back when he walks past me toward the raised area where my bed is.

I watch him grab his slacks and pull them on before picking up his shirt off the back of the chair in the corner and shrugging it on. I wrap my arms around my waist as he sits to put on his shoes, and then I hold my breath once he's done and stands. I wonder if I'm making a mistake as he walks toward me but remind myself that he lied, not once but numerous times. He could have come clean at any point last night, but he never did.

"Tomorrow I leave to head out of town for a few days," he states, and my stomach drops at that news. "When I get back, we'll talk."

"We won't." I hate the way my voice shakes.

He closes the distance between us then reaches out to touch me, but I move my head to the side before he can cup my cheek. His jaw twitches as his hand forms a fist as it drops to his side. "I'll see you soon."

I don't respond. I don't know how to. He stares at me for what seems like a lifetime before he finally turns to leave, and it isn't until the door closes behind him that I'm finally able to take a breath.

I take two steps, drop my elbows to the kitchen counter, and rest my face in my hands. I want to cry, not because I'm sad, but because I'm so mad at myself. I should have…. I don't know what I should have done, but I should have known Braxton wasn't who he claimed to be. I should have read between the lines and trusted my gut.

The moment I saw you, I wanted you.

Who says something like that? What kind of man even thinks something like that, let alone acts on it? Probably the same kind of man who wears a suit like second skin, drives a G-class Benz, and has a standing reservation at a place like Altura.

My phone ringing from the bathroom pulls me from my thoughts, and I suck in a breath before I push away from the counter. By the time I reach my cell, it's no longer ringing, but there's a missed call from Jamie on the screen. I don't want to call him back. I'm sure he's talked to Maggie and is wondering what the hell happened to me, but knowing he's worried forces me to dial his number.

"Dakota, what the fuck," he says in greeting, and I close my eyes.

"What the fuck what?" I ask, trying not to let him hear in my tone everything I'm feeling.

"I talked to Maggie. She told me you stood up your date, and then I haven't been able to get a hold of you. I was two minutes away from calling the cops, since the fucking people at your building wouldn't let me up to check on you."

Damn, I'm glad I didn't give him a key. "There's no need to come check on me. I'm fine. I just..." God,

I hate lying to him. "I just couldn't go through with meeting the guy she wanted me to… so I stood him up and…."

"You don't need to explain that to me. I was just worried about you," he says quietly then asks, "Are you home?"

"Yeah." I look around my bathroom, noting the sheet from my bed on the floor. I pick it up and take it with me to my bed, and with my phone in one hand, I rip the fitted sheet from the mattress and take it to the washer just beyond the kitchen.

"Do you want to eat dinner with me tonight before my show? I could get Chinese and bring it to you." My stomach turns as I shove my sheets into the washer.

"I have some work I need to do before Monday." It's not a lie. One of the products I will be selling Monday on air is making me nervous, since it's a product that hasn't been on the market long and how much I sell could determine if I get more well-known brands. "How about breakfast tomorrow?"

"Breakfast?" he asks like he's never heard of it before as I dump detergent into the machine.

I smile, knowing he is never up before noon after a show. "Okay, brunch—a late brunch."

"All right," he gives in, and I hear him let out a breath. "Are you sure you're okay?"

I close the lid on the washer, listening to it start. "I'm sure. Call me when you're up tomorrow, and let me know where you want to meet."

"All right, love you."

I smile at that and head to the kitchen, seeing the cup of coffee there. "Love you too." I hang up then dump what's left in the cup in the sink, grabbing a spoon from the drawer and my ice cream from the freezer. I take it with me to the couch and look over the back to the city just outside the window as I flip off the top. I scoop out one bite after another, letting the cold chocolate melt against my tongue and knowing it's time for me to give up on the idea of the white picket fence and Mr. Right.

Chapter 4

AN ANNOYING RINGING wakes me, and I fumble for my phone on my side table and force one eye open, trying to figure out how to shut it off. When I see the screen is black and realize the ringing isn't coming from my cell, I groan then roll out of bed. I stumble to the kitchen and press the green light that is flashing on the wall near the door, and my voice comes out raspy as I say, "Hello."

"Ms. Newton, are you available to receive a delivery?" a man asks, and I frown, glancing at the clock. A delivery at ten till eight on a Sunday?

"Can I ask what it is?"

"Flowers." He pauses then adds, "Lots of flowers."

Braxton. I close my eyes and sigh. "I'm available."

"We'll be right up." The line goes dead.

Figuring I have a few minutes, I head for my closet and change into a pair of high-waisted leggings and a sports bra then grab a hoodie. I put it on before grabbing my running shoes. Just as I finish tying them, there is a knock on the door, and as soon as I pull it open, my eyes widen.

There's not just one person carrying a single bouquet of roses, but six men and women, each holding two large vases. "Where should we put these?" the older man in front of the group asks.

"I guess anywhere you can find a free space." I step back out of his way and wave my hand out to encompass the room.

"Someone must really like you." One of the girls smiles as she walks past me, heading into the living room, since the kitchen island and counters have already been covered. I want to tell her she's wrong, but I keep my mouth shut, mumbling a quiet "thank you" as they start to leave.

Once they're gone, I close the door then lean back against it, taking in the multitude of different-colored roses now littering every free surface in my apartment. A card attached around one of the vases on the counter catches my attention, so I walk toward it and slowly detach it from the ribbon holding it secure. The small white card fits in the palm of my hand and is light as a feather, but it still feels like it weighs hundreds of pounds as I read the rough writing scrawled across the surface.

You were mine.

You'll be mine again. BA

I bite my lip and look around the room, unsure how to feel. Part of me is elated that Braxton didn't forget me the minute he left; another part of me is holding on to the anger of his deception. Needing to clear my head and figuring some fresh air might do me some good, I grab my key pass and leave my apartment, heading to the elevator and taking it down to the first floor. When I reach the lobby, I wave at the doorman as he opens the door for me and look both ways when I reach the sidewalk before I take off on a jog.

I pull my hoodie up over my hair when it starts to drizzle and run down the block toward the park, enjoying the cool breeze and even the mist as it brushes against my skin. Ten minutes into my run, I notice a black car with dark-tinted windows on the street seems to be following me. I shove my hands into my hoodie pocket for my cell just in case then bite back a curse when I don't find it and realize I left it next to my bed. The sidewalk is quiet; just a few people are out, so I follow my gut and turn left when I reach the end of the block, noting the car mirrors my move.

I pick up speed when I spot a drug store and dip inside, waiting at the door for the car to pass, but it doesn't. It stops right out front. With my heart pounding, I figure it will take them time to turn around if I head back to my building, so I exit when the next person enters and run at full speed down the block and around the corner. I don't even look to see if the car has turned around and I'm so focused on breathing and not tripping over my feet, I don't have time to stop when someone steps into my path. I barrel into them at full speed, hearing them grunt as they wrap their arms around me to keep me from taking us both to the ground.

"I'm sorry, so sorry." I place one hand against a hard chest and attempt to push away.

"Dakota."

No, it can't be.

I lift my head, coming face-to-face with Braxton.

"Are you okay?"

"W-What a… are you doing here?" I pant, trying to catch my breath.

"Why does it look like you've seen a ghost?" he asks, ignoring my question, and I look behind me then along the street to see if the car is there, but it's nowhere in sight.

"I…" I lick my lips, shaking my head knowing I just freaked myself out for no reason. "I haven't ran in a while," I lie, and the air around us seems to fill with electricity as I look into his eyes. "Why are you here? I thought you were going out of town?"

"I am." He glances toward the street, and I follow his gaze, noticing a silver SUV waiting near the curb with a large man standing outside near the driver door with his eyes on Braxton. "Did you get the flowers?" he asks, touching my cheek, and I focus on him then drop my eyes to his side and the suitcase there, putting two and two together.

"Do you live here?" I ask, taking a step away from him and watching his jaw twitch and his hand form a fist as it drops to his side.

"I do."

I nod, wrapping my arms around my middle, wondering why he never mentioned living in the building when I told him it's where I lived. Oh right—because he's a big, fat liar.

"Have a good trip." I turn to walk away as anger creeps up my spine.

"Dakota." He takes hold of my bicep, stopping me, and I look at him over my shoulder. "We'll talk." He skims his finger along my cheek, and I soak in the feeling of his touch then force myself to shrug off his hold. I head inside, feeling the heat of his gaze as I go to the elevator, but I don't turn to confirm he's watching me. When the doors open, I step inside then rest back against the wall and wait for them to shut.

Just as they're about to close, they are pried back open and Braxton appears with his chest heaving. I stare at him with wide eyes, unsure what to do or say as he stares back. When he steps toward me, my breath freezes in my lungs, and then before I can prepare, his body and mouth crash into mine. I react without thinking, sliding my fingers into his hair, and he groans. I whimper against his tongue when he lifts me off my feet and holds me against the wall, his hips locking me in place.

Even as my mind screams at me to push him away, I pull him closer, and his tongue flicks against mine while his hands on my ass urge me on. His scent and touch intoxicate me as desire surges between us like a wildfire burning out of control. Just when I'm about ready to beg him to take me to bed, he drags his mouth from mine and carefully lowers me to my feet. Panting now for a completely different reason, I blink my eyes open.

"I really fucking wish I didn't have to go." He captures my face between his palms, and mixed emotions go to war in my chest as he searches my gaze with a tender look.

"Th…" I drop my gaze and focus on his chin, unable to look him in the eye, and rest my hands against his chest. "That shouldn't have happened."

"It will inevitably happen between us again and again, Dakota."

Is he right? Probably. He seems to be my kryptonite. "You're a liar."

"I had a reason to lie." He smooths his thumb across my cheek.

"So you said, but then again, you didn't have a reason not to tell me that you live in the same building as me."

"That's a little more complicated." Now what the hell does that mean? "When I get back, I'll explain everything."

"Sure," I agree, hoping he'll let me go so I can remind myself why I'm mad at him—something that isn't easy with his hands holding me like he doesn't want to let go.

He smiles down at me like he knows exactly what I'm thinking. "I know where you live and where you work, Dakota."

"Why does that sound like a threat, Braxton?"

He brushes his lips across mine. "Because it is." He steps back, taking his warmth with him, then just as quickly as he appeared, he's gone and the doors close, leaving me alone once more. When the elevator buzzes, I quickly press the button for my floor then lean back against the wall, lifting my fingers to my lips that are still tingling. I don't know how to feel, but I do know Braxton was right. If we are around each other, what happened will inevitably happened again, and part of me wants it to.

Lord, I'm so screwed.

I GLANCE DOWN at my phone to check the time and get even more annoyed than I already am when I see Jamie's fifteen minutes late to meet me, even though he's the one who told me what time he'd be here. I look into the diner and debate going in to get a table then jump and scream when arms wrap around me from behind and I'm lifted off the ground.

"It's just me." Jamie laughs, dropping me to my feet.

I spin around and smack him on the arm. "You scared me."

"I kinda gathered that by the way you screamed." He chuckles as he wraps his arm around my shoulders and uses his free hand to open the door. "Are you ready to eat?"

"I was ready to eat fifteen minutes ago." I glare up at him.

"Sorry about that. I had company who didn't want to leave."

My nose scrunches. "Thank goodness I don't have to deal with your—" I lift my fingers, making quotations. "—company anymore."

"Oh come on, admit it. You miss me," he says as we slide into an open booth across from each other.

"You, yes. Your company? Not so much."

He grins then his expression turns serious. "Are you settling in all right?"

I let out a long breath then admit, "It's taking me time to get used to living on my own." I unwrap my silverware from my napkin then smile. "But I like my place and my job so far."

"Good." His eyes fill with relief, and I realize then he's been worried about me. "Have you made any friends at work?"

"Not yet, but I've only been there a week. I'm still trying to find where I fit in."

"You will, just give it time," he says, and then we both look at the waitress when she appears at the side of the table, holding a pot of coffee. Once she fills our cups, we give her our orders without even looking at the menu, because we've been here before and always order the same thing.

When she walks away, I mix sugar and creamer

into my coffee while asking, "How was your show last night?"

"Good. Really good. Dan showed after to go over our contract and to make sure we're set to hit the road in a few weeks."

"Are you ready for that?" I know becoming successful enough to go on tour has been his dream since we were kids, but dreaming about something and the reality of it happening can be vastly different.

"As ready as I'm gonna be. Dan keeps warning us that what's about to happen is going to change things for us and we need to be prepared."

"I'm worried about you," I tell him honestly. "I wish I could go with you."

"Maybe you can fly out when I'm in Nashville. We'll be there for a week after our first song off the new album goes live."

"I'd love that. I've always wanted to go to Nashville. Let me know the dates and I'll see if I can fly out for the weekend."

"I'll have Dan send you an e-mail with our tour schedule."

"Oh, Dan will send me an e-mail? How very famous of you. Should I also get your personal assistant's number so I can message her when I need to speak to you?"

"Smartass." He grins, and I grin back, but then his smile fades away. "So, do you wanna tell me what happened Friday?"

I almost choke on my coffee. I don't know why I

thought he'd let me get off not telling him about that. "Nope, not really."

His eyes narrow and I shift in my seat. "Talk."

"About what?"

"Dakota, I can read you like a book. I have always been able to, so spit it out. What happened that you don't want me to know about?"

"Nothing happened." I lift my thumb to my mouth, and he reaches across the table, tapping it away from my lips.

"What happened with the suit Maggie was trying to hook you up with?"

"I didn't meet up with him."

"I know you didn't. I also know you, and know you wouldn't stand someone up, which makes me think something happened to keep you from meeting him."

"Fine." I sigh. "I was going to meet him, but I was running late. Then there was an accident and the cab I was in couldn't get me across town, and I kinda figured it was a sign that I shouldn't go."

"You're lying," he states then waves his hand out to cut me off when I start to tell him I'm not. Which, I'm not. Well… mostly not, anyway. "I'm not upset you stood the guy up. I met him, and he reminded me of Troy."

"Really?" I scowl, not liking the idea of more than one Troy running around in the world.

"Yeah," he says then frowns over my shoulder, and I turn to see what he's looking at and notice a big guy sitting at a lone table reading the paper.

"Do you know him?" I ask, turning back to Jamie.

He focuses on me and shakes his head. "No, but he keeps looking over here like he knows me."

"Maybe he does. I mean, you are famous after all." I wink, and he laughs.

Just then, the waitress appears at our table with our food. We dig in and chat while we eat, and then when we're finished, he pays the tab and we head out.

"Do you still have a lot of work to do?" he asks when we stop on the sidewalk outside the dinner.

"I have a few things to do tonight, but nothing that will take me long."

"Then let's go see a movie, that comedy you wanted to see with that girl is out."

"You basically just described every comedy out right now." I laugh, lacing my arm through his. "A movie sounds good, and you can buy me popcorn and M&M's."

"I just bought you breakfast." He looks down at me as we walk down the block toward his SUV parked on the street.

"I know, but now were going to the movies, so I'm going to need a snack."

"Fine." He beeps the locks then opens the door for me to get in. Once he's behind the wheel, he starts the engine. I pull out my cell from my bag when it beeps with a message and frown when I see Braxton's name on the screen. "Is that Troy?" Jamie asks.

"No, my boss," I lie, opening the screen and going to the app for the theater, wondering when the hell

Braxton had a chance to program his number into my phone.

"Your boss is messaging you on a Sunday?"

"Yeah, she's just making sure I'm ready for the show Monday."

"I could never fucking work in the business world."

"Why, because you couldn't sleep in everyday and party all night?"

"Basically." I hear the smile in his voice as I purchase our tickets for a show that starts in thirty minutes. "So, have you talked to Troy?"

I shove my phone in my bag even though I really want to read the text waiting for me. "He sent a text in the middle of the week telling me that he would be in Seattle in a couple weeks and wants to meet up."

"You're not going to meet with him, are you?" I hear the annoyance in his tone.

"I don't want to, but he said he has a box I left in the closet, and I know after getting my stuff from storage that it's a box of photos of me, you, and Mom, and I'd like them back."

"Tell him to fucking mail them."

"I would, but I'm worried if I do, he might just toss them in the trash," I say quietly, having no doubt he would do that just to be vindictive.

"I'll go get them for you."

"Jamie." I sigh. "I'm going to meet him somewhere. I'm not going to dinner with him or out on a date. You need to give me some credit."

"I know you don't want to be with him, Dakota, but

I know he's a smooth talker, and that fucking guy will use whatever he can to get you alone so he can try to convince you that he is a changed man and to take him back."

I want to tell him that he's wrong, but since I left, Troy has been finding reasons for me to meet up with him. The other times, I was able to avoid seeing him, but this time, I can't just send an e-mail or make a phone call to get things sorted out.

"Fine, I'll see if he can mail me the box," I give in, but I know that if he says he won't send them or can't, I will be forced to meet up with him. I don't have any desire to see Troy, but I do want my photos. I don't have much from Jamie's and my childhood, but in that box are photos of some of the better times in our lives and the few pictures of my parents I have.

"Just promise me that if you do have to meet up with him, you'll let me know so I can go with you." God, my brother seriously knows me so well.

"Promise," I say as he pulls in to park in the movie theater parking lot. Once we get inside, they scan my cell for the tickets then we head to the concession stand. After we get our stuff, I stop to add extra butter to my popcorn, and a tingle hits the back of my neck. I glance around, swearing I recognize the guy from the diner before he disappears into the men's bathroom.

"Ready?" Jamie asks, and I turn to find him carrying a drink and a few different types of candy.

"Yep." I shake off the feeling in the pit of my stomach and head in to find our seats. Then, like always when I'm with my brother, all the drama and bullshit disappears and I just enjoy spending some time laughing with him.

Chapter 5

DAKOTA

"*H*OLD THE ELEVATOR," I yell as I push the cart in front of me as fast as I can, blushing in embarrassment as one of the wheels squeaks obnoxiously loud. It causes people to stop what they're doing and watch me make my way across the lobby floor toward the closing silver doors. A large, tan hand and a wrist sporting a fancy watch swings out just in time, keeping the door open. Sighing in relief, I wheel the cart into the elevator then pick up my cell phone so I can look at the e-mail Kathy sent me and confirm what floor I'm supposed to go to.

"What floor?" a gravelly voice asks, a voice that has the hairs on the back of my neck standing on end as the scent of familiar dark musk wraps around me.

Lifting my eyes away from my phone, my throat

closes up and my pulse quickens as I take in the imposing figure beside me. Even in my four-inch heels, his height towers over my five-six frame. His navy-blue suit does amazing things for his eyes, and the black tie around his neck screams power. Fidgeting, my eyes move up to meet his mint-green ones and I notice a familiar glimmer of desire and anger.

"What floor?" he asks again as his strong, angled jaw tics.

"Forty-seven, please," I say quietly like I'm afraid he will attack if I speak too loud, and he might. I remember what happened the last time we were in an elevator together.

Nodding, his eyes leave mine and he presses my number then waves his wrist over the screen. The number sixty flashes briefly before disappearing, making me wonder if that's a floor in this building, because the numbers only go up to fifty on the panel. Crossing his arms over his chest, I take in his short, dark, almost-black hair and tan skin. He's somehow become even better looking since the last time I saw him, and that should be impossible. Then again, he also shouldn't be here.

"Dakota, you should know it's rude to stare," he states then inhales through his nose and his hands tighten into fists as his jaw grinds.

"What are you doing here, Braxton?" I know the answer without asking, and the anger that had dissipated with every text he's sent me while he's been away comes back full force.

"I think you know."

"Yeah." My throat gets tight with the urge to scream. "Why?" The question is barely audible. I don't get it. I don't understand why he hasn't told me the truth even once since we've known each other.

"It's complicated," he mutters, sweeping his eyes over me from head to toe, bringing every cell in my body to life in that one look, before facing the door when it opens and people step on. I wrap my hands around the handle of my cart and squeeze, feeling his eyes on me, but I don't turn to look at him. On the next floor, the few people who got on step off, leaving us alone again.

"You haven't returned any of my messages."

I haven't. I've wanted to, but I haven't. Now I'm glad I stayed strong. The one this morning telling me he just landed in Seattle was especially difficult to ignore.

"We'll talk tonight and I'll explain things to you."

"We won't, I don't need you to explain anything," I say as the elevator stops. I get off even though it's not my floor and my legs shake as I push through the crowd waiting to get on. Once the doors close, I press the button and wait for the next one to come, hoping I don't have to quit my job.

When I finally make it to the forty-seventh floor, I head for the conference room and find the door open. "Good, you're here." Kathy sighs dramatically, helping me drag the cart to the corner of the room. Since I started working with Kathy, I've noticed she's more often than not dramatic in everything she does. "Mr. Adams wasn't supposed to be back until next week, but he flew in this morning and wants us to hold the new merchandise meeting now," she says, picking up a stack of papers and handing them to me, and I wonder how it's possible she has no idea I'm currently having a heart attack.

I'm sure there are other men with the last name Adams. But it's too much of a coincidence to think that the CEO and Braxton who have the same last name both flew in this morning. She bends over and unlocks the doors on the cart with a key tethered around her wrist and pulls out a dozen or more small boxes that are enclosed in a large plastic bag. "Each place gets a pamphlet and a box except that chair there." She nods toward the head of the table, where a bottle of water is sitting unopened.

"Got it." I take the boxes from her and set them on the table.

"Thank you for helping me with this, I'll be back in ten minutes. I need coffee. Can you handle this until I get back?"

"Of course, go." I shoo her away, needing a minute alone to wrap my head around things. I begin the mindless task of placing the pamphlets and boxes around the table and play out every scenario in my head. Most of them end with me quitting and living with Jamie again—something I don't really want to do but will. When I hear the door open, I don't even look up, assuming Kathy's come back.

"Glad to see you made it here, since you got off on the wrong floor," Braxton says, and I jump, turning to find him sitting at the head of the table and opening the bottle of water that was placed there.

"So, I'm guessing this is where you tell me this is your company?" I prompt as my stomach turns and my hands start to shake.

"I told you it was complicated."

"For once, you didn't lie," I say sarcastically, wanting to toss the box in my hand at his stupid head.

"I haven't lied to you," he states, leaning back in the chair and resting his ankle on his knee.

"No, you've just kept the truth to yourself until you didn't have a choice but to come clean."

"Braxton!" Kathy exclaims, breaking our stare-down, and we turn to watch her walk into the room with a cup of coffee in her hand and a smile on her face.

"Kathy." He stands to greet her with a kiss to her cheek.

"How was your trip? Did you and Hanna enjoy your time?" she asks, and his posture changes ever so slightly.

"It was business, Kathy," he states quietly but firmly.

"I may be old, but I remember what it's like to be young and—"

"Kathy," he cuts her off, letting the warning in his tone hang in the air between them. What she's implying registers, and that knot in my stomach moves to fill my chest. Lord in heaven, not only is he a liar; he's a cheater. Why do I have such shit luck when it comes to men?

"Fine, fine." She waves her hand around between them. "Did you have a chance to introduce yourself to Dakota?"

He turns toward me, and the look in his eyes is filled with an uncomfortable amount of familiarity. I silently beg him not to say that we know each other.

"Nice to meet you, Dakota." He steps toward me, and I brace as he holds out his hand.

"Nice to meet you too, Mr. Adams." I place my hand in his, despising the tingles that shoot up my arm and travel through my blood stream. I try to remove my hand from his, but his grip is firm. He smiles a devastating smile, one that shows off perfectly straight teeth and a slight dimple in his right cheek, a dimple I didn't notice until now. I let out the breath I was holding when he finally releases me and moves back to the head of the table where he was seated before.

I go back to what I was doing, ignoring the heat I feel coming from his direction and his and Kathy's quiet conversation. Once I'm finished, I start to head for the door, needing to get out of the room.

"Come take a seat, Dakota," he says as my hand lands on the doorknob, and my shoulders sag.

I look over my shoulder and watch Kathy shake her head. "She's not sitting in on this meeting. I just needed her help getting things set up."

"Come sit down," he repeats, staring at me and

silently daring her to dispute him again. Knowing I need this job and that I don't want to embarrass Kathy or myself, I walk toward the table as he pushes out the chair next to him. Taking the seat, I cross one leg over the other, unsure of what to do, because Kathy—who has always seemed to like me—is looking at me like she wants to remove my head with the pen in her hand. "Kathy, can you go make sure everyone is ready for the meeting?"

"Of course, Braxton," she murmurs as she stands, giving me a strange look before walking across the room to the door and closing it behind herself.

"I need this job," I hiss when his eyes come to me. "I don't know what just happened, but I like Kathy, I like working here, and I need this job."

Leaning across me, he ignores my statement and picks up the box in front of me on the table and opens it, pulling out a watch that looks similar to his and unclasping the band.

"Where's your phone?"

"Why?"

"Let me see it." He holds out his hand, so I give it to him without thinking and he taps it to the watch then a moment later, he looks at me. "Give me your hand."

"Why?" I repeat and clasp my hands together in my lap, and his eyes flash with something I don't understand, something that scares me but at the same time makes me feel butterflies in the pit of my stomach. Without answering my question, he pulls my hands apart, his fingers wrapping tightly around my wrist, not enough to cause pain but tight enough that I know it would be useless to try to get free. Working quickly, he buckles the wristwatch in place and then taps his wrist to mine, causing the watch to light up and flash in some strange code that is matching the one flashing on his.

"What is this?" I ask, studying the device that is now wrapped firmly around my wrist.

"It's a watch that connects to your phone. It's an IMG exclusive device, that links with all our products."

"I don't want it," I tell him, tugging free from his hold. I start to pull at the band of the watch to remove it but freeze when he grabs my hand.

"Do not take it off," he orders, making my spine stiffen as my eyes fly up to meet his.

"You're freaking me out," I breathe in distress as my chest begins rising and falling rapidly from the look in his eyes.

"Why?" His brows pull together like he doesn't understand how I could possibly be freaked out, but everything in me is telling me to get up and run as fast as I can. I don't even know how to begin to explain to someone like him that they are being overbearing, when it seems to be ingrained in his DNA.

"You just are." I let my hands fall to my lap with the watch still in place.

"I'd never hurt you," he says as his eyes soften, and it looks like he wants to say more, but before he can, the door to the room opens and people begin to filter in. They look between him and me with curiosity as they take their seats around the table.

I pull the sleeve of my silk blouse over the watch and catch Kathy's eye as she takes her seat. Unease fills me when I see the distrust in her gaze, but I just smile, playing stupid.

"Do I need to stay for this?" I ask her quietly, and Braxton grabs my thigh under the table. When she shakes her head, I quickly get up and leave without a backward glance. I take the elevator down to the fourth floor, and as soon as I reach my desk, I touch my finger to the screen of the watch, and it lights up with an image of a digital clock. I press the buttons on the side, and the screen changes to a digital calendar. I press it again, and I see my office e-mail account, and when I press it one more time, my text messages show up.

I let my hand fall to my lap, then try to focus on studying the information I need to know for a new device from IMG that will be airing tomorrow. A device that will allow you to do everything from make appointments, purchase event tickets, order groceries or take out, to maintain your home security. All things most people do today with different apps or devices, but with this, you can do it all in one place. IMG isn't the first to come out with a home portal, but like a lot of their branded devices it's built to work with all other IMG products, and I'm guessing the watch on my wrist will be soon added to their list.

I get to work, hoping that the talking points I come up with will appeal to not only younger people but older people as well, showcasing just how easy the device is to set up and use. When the phone on my desk buzzes, I pick it up, putting it to my ear. "Dakota Newton."

"Dakota, can you please come into my office and bring me a coffee on the way?" Kathy asks, and my chest instantly fills with anxiety.

"Absolutely, I'll be right there," I say, trying to sound cheerful even though I might pass out. I stop at the kitchen and use the machine to make a cup of coffee then take it with me to Kathy's office on the other side of the floor.

I tap on her open door when I reach it, and enter when she calls, "Come in."

"Did you need something?" I ask, setting the cup on the edge of the desk when she doesn't speak.

She leans back in her chair, locking her fingers together over her stomach. "I'm curious about something."

Oh, God, here it is.

"Curious?" I parrot.

"Did you know Braxton before I introduced you?"

"Know him?" I shake my head. "No, I didn't know him." I shift on my feet and barely stop myself from wringing my hands together. "I mean, I ran into him in the elevator this morning, but I didn't really talk to him." I hope the half-lie will explain my nervousness and what happened upstairs.

"He spoke to me about moving you upstairs to work side by side with Chris Stines, who runs the marketing department for IMG."

My stomach bottoms out. "What? But I don't know anything about marketing," I tell her, something she already knows.

"I explained that to him, but he's under the impression you would be a better fit working with that team."

"Tell him I don't feel comfortable with the responsibility working in that department would entail," I plea, and her eyes soften for the first time since we were in the conference room. I don't know what Braxton's reasoning is for wanting to move me, but I doubt it's anything that would make me happy. And since I have gotten through most of my life by trusting my instincts and every one of them is screaming at me to avoid him, I'm going to do that.

"I'll see what I can do," she mutters, picking up the coffee I set down and taking a sip. "Why don't you go get lunch while I make a few calls? When you get back, I'll go over what you have so far for the show tomorrow."

My muscles relax. "Sure, would you like anything from the deli?"

"I think you've noticed I survive on coffee most days."

"In that case, I'll bring you a sandwich," I say, gaining a smile before I turn for the door.

Going to my desk, I grab my purse, slip off my heels, and put on my flats then head for the elevator. Once I reach the lobby floor and head out of the building, I unconsciously look down at my wrist and frown when I notice in the corner a tiny red light is blinking slowly. Walking quickly to the deli at the end of the block, I head right for the bathroom, where I take the watch off and drop it in the trash next to the sink. After washing my hands, I leave the bathroom feeling lighter.

I walk two more blocks to another deli and go to the counter, where I order a turkey and Swiss on rye and take a seat in the back of the restaurant. I pull out my phone and pull up my messages, ignoring the ones from Braxton and responding to Jamie's text about dinner.

"Did you lose something?" a familiar deep voice asks as the seat in front of me scrapes against the floor, and I look up then watch Braxton fold his large frame into the small chair. Then he drops the watch on the table between us.

"No," I mumble, looking back down at my phone when it vibrates with an incoming text from Jamie saying he'll bring dinner to my place around six.

I start to text him back, but Braxton's fingers move to my jawline pressing up until my eyes meet his. "I want you to wear the watch."

"I don't want to wear your tracking device," I tell him with a shrug as my heartbeat picks up. "That's what it is, right?" I mean, I'm not sure, but that's the only thing I can think it might be.

"I don't need to track you, Dakota. You live in my building." He leans across the table closer to me, and my heart that was already thumping hard begins to pound. "You work for my company. I know almost everything about you. You can't avoid me."

"What do you want from me?"

"A chance," he says easily as his thumb runs along the edge of my bottom lip. My eyes slide to half-mast and I lean into his touch. "You can't deny our connection."

Swallowing, I pull away from him and sit back in my chair, unsure how he has the power to make me forget everything with a simple touch. I look away from him and wrap my arms around my middle. He's right; I can't deny our connection. It's like a living, breathing thing that's taken on a life of its own. "A chance to what… lie to me some more?" I shake my head. "No, thank you."

"I wanted to tell you the truth."

"You should have told me the truth. You could have told me the truth." I uncross my arms and point at him. "You chose to lie to me."

"You're right." He leans back and runs his fingers through his hair. "You're right; I should have told you, but I didn't, because I saw what I wanted and wasn't going to let anything get in the way of me getting it— including you."

Again. Seriously? "You cannot be believed."

"Tell me this." He sits forward, resting his elbows on the table. "If I told you when you came up to me on the street that I wasn't Adam, would you have let me take you to dinner?"

Of course not.

Maybe.

Crap, I honestly don't know. Instead of answering his question, I ask, "Who is Hanna?"

"No one."

I raise a brow. "Kathy made it seem like she's someone to you."

"She's Kathy's niece. We went out a few times. It was never serious."

"And you work with her?" I prompt, because I know Kathy said she was on his trip with him.

I watch him closely to see if he's lying—not that I would know if he is or not. "We do work together, she's my assistant." He looks down at my sandwich and pushes it closer to me. "Eat."

My nose wrinkles, not because I don't want to eat, but because he's telling me to. "Don't annoy me by telling me what to do right now."

"If I remember correctly, you like me telling you what to do," he says in a tone that makes my skin seem to vibrate and my toes curl.

I pick up my sandwich and take a bite just for something to do, and he chuckles. After I chew and swallow, I wipe my mouth with my napkin and go back to the topic of Hanna, unwilling to let the subject go. Not because of the jealousy that's building in the pit of my stomach, but because I just want to know. "It must be awkward working with your ex."

"She's not my ex."

I roll my eyes. "Okay, someone you slept with."

"Our relationship has never been anything but

professional. We went out but neither of us felt anything more than friendship for the other."

"I'm sure." I let out a breath, unsure if I'm even comfortable with the way I'm feeling right now, even if I don't have any right to feel upset.

"Did Kathy tell you that I want to move you upstairs?"

"She did." I ball up the napkin I'm still holding and toss it onto my sandwich, my appetite completely gone. "I told her that I don't want to move."

"I saw some of the work you've done, Dakota."

"If I wanted a job in marketing, I would have applied for it." I hold his stare, silently daring him to use the power he has to do whatever he wants despite me telling him not to move me.

With a sigh, he shakes his head. "If you change your mind, the job is yours."

"Thanks." I pick up my phone and check the time. It feels like I've been sitting here with him forever, but it's only been about twenty minutes, which means I still have about thirty minutes before I have to get back to the office. Just as I'm about to stand and excuse myself, my phone rings in my hand and the watch on the table vibrates. When I see it's Troy calling, I wonder what I did recently that I need to repent for. Unwilling to talk to him, I end the call by sending a message saying I'm busy and will call back.

"Who's Troy?" Braxton asks, and I look at him.

"My ex-fiancé." I don't know if I tell him because I want him to realize he doesn't know everything about me or if I just want to see his reaction. And he does react—his jaw instantly gets tight and he looks down at the watch between us like he wants to take it outside and run it over. Before he can do that, I pick it up. "Thanks for the watch." I scoot away from the table to stand. "I'm sure I'll see you around."

"We will definitely be seeing each other." He stands and blocks me so I can't get past him. "I'll be at your place tonight."

"I have plans tonight."

"With your brother?" I'm not sure if it's a question or if he's letting me know he's aware I have plans with Jamie. "Like I said, I'll see you tonight." He leans down, touching his lips to my cheek, and all I can do is stand there and soak in the feeling of his lips on me like a complete idiot.

Chapter 6

DAKOTA

$\mathcal{S}$ITTING ON THE floor in front of the coffee table, I pick up my glass of wine and take a sip. Since Jamie left an hour ago, I've been reviewing the notes Kathy left for me, and I'm finding it hard not to toss them into the trash. All of my hard work was for nothing. She didn't like any of my ideas. She might as well just write me a script to follow for tomorrows show or tie strings to my hands and control me like a puppet. With a tired groan, I rub my eyes then frown when my front door beeps. I look up as it starts to open, and my adrenalin spikes as I watch someone step inside, their features blocked by the shadows. I attempt to scoot under the coffee table but can barely get my head underneath it, so I settle with lying as still as I can while holding my breath.

"Dakota, I can see you."

Braxton.

I sit up quickly and curse myself when I accidentally bump my almost full glass of red wine, watching it tip over and fall on the white plush carpet. "Shit." I jump up and rush to the kitchen, dropping the glass in the sink. I grab a small towel and wet the edge of it then go back to the rug and attempt to use it to blot the stain away, but it doesn't work. If anything, I seem to be spreading it farther. "Great." I glare at the man now standing over me. "This rug probably cost thousands of dollars, and now I have to replace it because of you."

"It didn't cost thousands of dollars." His brow pulls together. "Or I don't think it did." He bends over and takes the rag from my hand. "And you don't need to replace it. I'll have the building manager take care of it."

Right. I roll my eyes. How could I forget he owns this building, and IMG, and he just walked right into my home like he owns it—because he kind of does? "How did you get in here?"

"You wear glasses?" he asks, ignoring my question, and I push my blue light glasses up the bridge of my nose then touch my hair, which is piled on top of my head in a messy bun.

I'm sure I look like a wreck, but I honestly didn't think I'd see him. My plan if he did show up tonight was to ignore him until he went away. So much for that.

I take off my glasses and toss them to the top of the

coffee table then cross my arms over my chest. "You didn't answer my question."

"I told you I'd be here."

"I didn't ask you why you're here. I asked you how you got into my place without a key, Braxton," I snap, and he sighs, taking a seat on the couch.

"If I tell you the truth, are you going to freak out?"

"Probably." I tap my foot, waiting for him to come clean.

"I linked your digital information with mine."

My nose scrunches. "And what does that mean?"

"It means all the information you have on your phone is now linked with mine, including the app to get into your apartment."

I fall to the couch, my ass on the edge of the seat, and rub my forehead. "I slept with an insane person."

"Dakota." His hand lands on my shoulder, and I pull away from his touch and turn on him.

"God, you're crazy." I hold up my hand when it looks like he's going to speak. "You need to go."

"Dakota."

"Why does everything with you have to be so over the top? Why can't you just be a normal guy?" I shake my head. "Who breaks into someone's apartment?"

"I didn't break in."

"No, you just used my information—information I didn't even give to you—to let yourself in." I fall back against the couch and groan. "I can't believe that when I met you, I thought you might be the perfect man. God, I suck at reading men."

"If I knocked on your door tonight, would you have answered?"

"Probably not." I turn my head toward him. "But it would have been my choice if I did. Just like it would have been my choice to stand up the guy I was supposed to go out with. That's the thing, Braxton; you can't just make decisions for people. You can't make decisions for me, just because you want to get your way."

"I like getting my way."

"Yeah, I know." I shake my head then watch him lean forward and pick up Kathy's notes from the coffee table.

"What's this?"

"I would say none of your business, but since it's your company, I can't, and I want to just let you know that's also really annoying."

He smiles, and I hate that my heart beats a little harder seeing it. God he really has put some kind of spell on me. Even as annoyed as I am by his highhandedness and the fact that he's a damn liar, I still can't be really mad at him.

"What's that look?"

"Nothing." I sigh, getting up from the couch, taking the red-stained rag from him, and carrying it toward the kitchen. "Do you want some tea?"

"Are you inviting me to stay?"

"If I ask you to leave again, are you going to listen to me and go?" He smirks, and I mutter, "I didn't think so." I hear him chuckle as I flip the switch on my electric teapot.

"Explain these notes to me." He holds up his hand holding the notes, before sitting forward so he can click through the talking points I created on my computer.

I inwardly groan. I don't want to explain Kathy's notes or why I'm annoyed with her, especially not to him. I might not like what she wants to do, but she is still my boss and I refuse to go behind her back. "They're just notes about the show tomorrow."

"I see that, Dakota," he says, sounding frustrated, and I inwardly smile, liking him frustrated.

'Then there is nothing to explain." I drop a chai spice teabag into my cup then cover it with steaming water a minute later.

"She doesn't like what you came up with," he says as I walk back to the couch. "Why?"

I shrug, not answering, taking a seat near the arm, as far away from him as I can be.

"You're really not going to talk to me about this?"

"Nope, I'm really not."

"So stubborn."

"Oh, isn't that just like the dalmatian calling a leopard spotted?"

"And a smartass." He drops the paper in his hand to the coffee table and leans back, making himself comfortable, placing his ankle to his knee and his arm along the back of the couch. I notice then that he's not in his usual suit but wearing dark slacks and a blue button-down shirt. "How was dinner with your brother?"

"Good." I take a sip of tea, and he taps his fingers on the back of the couch when I don't say more.

"Talk to me, Dakota."

"About what, Braxton?"

"I don't fucking care. I just want to hear you talk."

"I'm not in the mood to talk. My plans for the night didn't include a late-night guest. My plans included me having a glass of wine, which is now on the floor, doing some work, and then going to bed."

"We can go to bed."

I narrow my eyes. "Don't make me dump this very hot tea over your head. I'm still really pissed at you."

"How can I make you less pissed?" he asks, touching my shoulder with the tips of his fingers. Just that small touch makes me shiver and curse myself. "I apologized for lying. What else do you want me to do?"

"You kind of apologized, and then you stole my information and broke into my apartment," I remind him. "What would you do if someone did that to you?" I hold up my hand when it looks like he's going to respond. "And don't lie. You'd probably lose your mind."

"You're right—I would."

"Then don't you think I have the right to be mad?"

"You do, but—"

I cut him off with a groan. "You do know that the word 'but' means 'ignore everything I just said,' right? You are seriously the most frustrating man I have ever met in my life."

"Then we're on an even playing field, because I was just thinking the same thing about you."

"How am I frustrating you? Because I'm not just letting you off the hook? It wasn't me, Braxton, who got into this relationship under false pretenses then lied and lied some more."

"Relationship?" He raises one brow.

"Don't even go there," I hiss. "You know exactly what I mean."

"I'd like to be in a relationship with you."

"And I'd like to kill you, but I doubt I could get away with it without someone coming to look for you."

I watch him laugh then brace when his expression turns serious. "You should know I'm not going to stop pursuing you until you give me another chance."

God, he's relentless. "Are you an only child?"

"No, I have two sisters and a brother."

"That's surprising."

"I'm not some spoiled brat who's used to getting their way, Dakota. I'm a man who knows what he wants. And when I find something I want, I go after it until it belongs to me."

"Again, Braxton, I'm a person, not an object you can own."

"You're right, but that doesn't mean you can't belong to me."

Lord, his overbearingness should not turn me on, but there is no denying the way his words make me feel.

"And you have to know that if you belong to me,

I'd belong to you as well."

"Braxton."

"You want me, Dakota. I know you do. You might be trying to push me away, but you don't actually want me to go."

He's right, isn't he? I could have done something when he broke in, but I didn't, and I haven't done much to make him leave. I like his company; I like the way he looks at me, and even when he's annoying me, I like being around him. I know I shouldn't, but that doesn't change that I do.

"I need time."

"How much time do you need?"

"I don't know. Am I going to find out anything else about you that I don't know?"

"There's a lot about me you don't know."

"See? That right there is what puts me on edge," I say, pulling my legs under me on the couch. "Everything you say leaves lots of room for you to come back later and sideswipe me."

"How's that?" He looks genuinely confused.

"I asked if there is anything else I don't know about you, and your answer is there's a lot. Lots, like what? A wife, a kid… are you running for president or planning to take over the world?"

"No wife, no kids. If I did have a wife, I wouldn't cheat on her. I don't want to be president, and I have no desire to take over the world. You know the big stuff about me. I own IMG, this building, and I'm obsessed with a woman I tricked into going on a date with me."

I stare at him, unsure what to say or how to respond. Part of me wants to give in and agree to see him, but I need time to figure out if he can be trusted. I still feel betrayed by him. He didn't just lie; he kept things from me and did it with ease. And if he did it once, he could do it again, and if that happened, it would be my fault. Like the old saying goes—fool me once, shame on you; fool me twice, shame on me.

"I'll give you time, Dakota, but you're not going to figure out if you can trust me unless you actually give me a chance to prove to you that you can."

"Can you read my mind?" I ask, honestly a little freaked he knows exactly what I'm thinking.

"No, but I'm beginning to understand the thing holding you back isn't that you don't want to spend time with me; it's that you don't trust me." He reaches out, touching my cheek. "Am I right?"

"Yeah."

His expression softens. "How about we take things slow?"

"What exactly do you mean by that?" Knowing him, his version of slow and mine are probably completely different.

"We spend time together, but nothing more until you're ready for that."

"Are we talking about sex?" Well that will be a challenge, maybe not for him but for me. I'm not sure I have enough willpower to spend time with him and not want what I know he's capable of making me feel.

"As much as it's going to kill me to keep my hands

off you, yeah, I mean sex." His eyes darken, and I squirm as they travel over my face. "But…"

"Here we go." I roll my eyes while smiling.

"But," he repeats, capturing my chin between his thumb and index finger then growls, "if you tempt me and start playing with fire, all bets are off."

My toes curl and my belly melts. "I'd never do that."

"Liar."

I am lying. Part of me wants to see how far I can push him before he cracks and just how hot it will be when he does.

"I also want you to join me for lunch with my parents this weekend."

Wait… what? "What?" My voice sounds shrill, even to my own ears. "How did we go from talking about me pushing you to a point where you can't control yourself to you telling me that you want me to meet your parents?"

Oh my God, here we go—right back on the crazy train.

"No way."

"No way?" He frowns, and I shake my head franticly.

"I can't meet your parents. I…. No way."

"Why not?"

"Um, I don't know. Maybe…" I hold up my hand and one finger. "Because you're my boss." I hold up another finger. "Because your parents." I hold up the rest of my fingers then let my hand drop to my lap. "Lots of reasons." His lips start to twitch, and I scowl at him when he starts to laugh. "Why are you laughing?"

"Because you're adorable when you're nervous, and this is the first time I've seen you really nervous about anything."

"I'm not nervous."

"Then what do you call it?"

"A normal reaction to someone you had a one-night stand with asking you to meet their parents."

"We didn't have a one-night stand."

"What?" I ask, caught off guard by the amount of anger in his tone and the way his fist clenches.

"We didn't have a fucking one-night stand."

"We did."

"We did fucking not."

"Why are you so pissed about this?"

"A one-night stand is someone you never see again, Dakota, the complete fucking opposite of what this is."

"Okay," I give in, because I can see how angry the topic is making him. "I'm just saying I don't think it's wise at this point in time for me to meet your parents."

"And I'm saying it is." He rips his hand through his hair.

"Can I think about it?" I bite my lower lip and fight the urge to laugh. I know this isn't funny, but at the same time his frustration is kind of adorable. He's so used to always getting his way that when he doesn't, he doesn't know how to react or act.

"Why does it look like you want to laugh?"

"Umm… because I do." I pat his hand still resting on the back of the couch. "You're so used to getting your way with everything that you don't know how to respond when you don't, and it's kind of funny."

"Don't piss me off, Dakota." He captures my wrist then pulls me toward him so we're face-to-face. "All that does is make me want to fuck you."

Damn, I want that. My eyes drop to his mouth. Maybe I should suggest we alter his rule just a tiny bit to involve orgasms.

"We could—"

"No," he cuts me off before I can say more and touches his lips to my forehead before pushing me back. "Even if this slow bullshit kills me, I'm going to give it to you."

Now why does that make me feel all warm and gooey inside?

"Tomorrow, dinner at my place. I'll cook for you and we'll talk." He stands like he's going to leave, and I want to ask him not to go but somehow manage not to.

"What floor do you live on?" I ask, not even pretending I'm not going to have dinner with him. Again, I might be an idiot, but I do like this man, even if he does make me insane and frustrates me to no end.

"What floor do you think I live on?"

"Yeah, that was a stupid question." I roll my eyes.

He smiles then leans over me to touch his hand to my cheek. "And that watch I gave you works both ways, so you can use it to get up to my place and let yourself in."

"That's a lot of trust. How do you know I'm not going to come up and steal all your silver?"

"I don't own any silver, and anything you see that you want, you can have, except the art my mom painted. She'd lose her mind if she came over and didn't see it where she hung it."

"That's sweet," I say while his thumb rubs across my cheek.

"She can't paint to save her life, but she's convinced it's good. I guess we all do what's necessary to keep the people in our lives happy."

"That's even sweeter," I reply, and he smiles slightly then bends at the waist. I hold my breath as he brushes his lips across mine, and when he pulls back, my lashes flutter open.

"I'll see you tomorrow evening. I'll be out of the office all day or I'd say we could have lunch."

"I think it's better if we keep things on the low," I tell him, covering his hand with mine and hoping he doesn't get mad. "I really don't want people to get the wrong impression, especially since I just started."

He drags in a breath through his nose and nods once. "I can give you that for now."

"Thank you."

"Anything." He lets me go and heads for the door. "Be good."

I have to laugh. "I'm always good."

"I doubt that." He winks then he disappears. After the door closes, I look over my shoulder at the view of the city lit up and smile when I realize I might be just as insane as Braxton Adams, and I'm okay with that.

Chapter 7

DAKOTA

*W*ITH A BOTTLE of water in hand, I head down to the gym to get in a run before I have to go to work, already dreading the idea of running. I'm not one of those people who enjoys working out, but I am one of those people who likes sweets and wine, so I pay my dues.

Once I step into the gym, I take off my sweatshirt and put it and my bottle of water into one of the lockers before going to the back of the room where the treadmills are lined up to look out over the city which is still dark. I hop on one near the end of the line, next to an older man who's walking while watching something on his iPad in front of him. I put in my headphones and turn up my music before starting up the machine, keeping my pace slow while I try to talk myself into going faster. After a couple minutes, I look to my left when someone gets on the machine next to mine—a redhead with a full face of makeup and her hair in a perfect ponytail. She waves, so I wave back wondering why she would waste time with makeup if she's just going to sweat it off.

I look at my reflection in the glass before me. Heck, I didn't even bother brushing my hair this morning; I just piled it on top of my head in a messy bun. I press the up arrow on the machine for it to go faster then notice the redhead looking my way, so I turn toward her again but see she's actually looking around me. I turn to check on the old guy, and my feet below me falter when I see a shirtless Braxton wearing sweats that should be outlawed while jogging, with his arms pumping and his muscles flexing.

He looks over at me and winks, making my skin warm. I want to ask him what he's doing here, but that would be a stupid question. It's a gym, and he's obviously working out. I play it cool and focus on keeping my feet under me and eyes straight ahead, and lucky me, I'm still able to watch him in the glass, just like what the redhead at my side is doing. I turn toward her, and she narrows her eyes on me. I guess the whole women's liberation business only lasts until there's a hot guy around.

I see her speed up her machine, so I do the same, and when she presses her arrow up again, I do too, which is stupid, because I might actually die while she doesn't even seem to be breathing heavy.

Refusing to embarrass myself, I slow down my machine to a jog then squeak a moment later when I'm lifted off my feet then set on solid ground. I lift my eyes off Braxton's bare chest and meet his gaze with the song "Bad Guy" roaring in my ears. The song fits him and the dark possessive look in his eyes. My chest rises and falls as he lifts his hand to my cheek and smooths his fingers back, tugging my ear bud from my ear. "Morning."

"Morning," I say, telling myself the breathy tone in my voice is because I just ran a mile, not because Braxton is standing so close, looking like he wants to devour me.

"Since you're done with your workout, wanna have breakfast with me?" His fingers brush mine, but my attention is pulled from him when I hear a loud noise behind me. I bite my lip, trying not to laugh as the redhead attempts to get her feet back under her and slow down. "You're so bad," Braxton whispers close to my ear, and I shiver, turning my head and coming face-to-face with him.

I drop my eyes to his mouth and lick my lips. "Breakfast sounds good."

"Come on." He takes my hand, but I stop him before he can pull me away. I turn off my machine, and then—because I'm petty—I shrug at the redhead and smirk, a silent *sorry not sorry, he's mine.*

"What?" I ask Braxton when he chuckles, but he just shakes his head.

We stop at the lockers, and I grab my sweatshirt

and bottle of water as he grabs a large black duffle bag before taking my hand once more. I let him lead me to the elevator, and he releases my hand to turn his back to me and wave his wrist across the screen. I put on my hoodie, leaving it unzipped, and lean against the wall as the doors close, holding my breath because I'm unsure what to expect as he turns to face me.

"Where is the watch I gave you?"

"I gave it to my brother," I reply, and his eyes narrow slightly. "What? I might have agreed to keep it, but I didn't tell you what I would do with it, and I wanted Jamie to be able to get into my place."

"Hmm." He skims his finger along the top edge of my sports bra, and I automatically grab onto the rail to keep myself standing. "Do you always work out dressed like this?"

"Why?"

"Curious." He slides his finger between my breasts and up my throat to my chin, taking it between his thumb and pointer finger.

"Braxton?"

He lowers his head toward mine. "Yeah?"

"Are you going to kiss me?"

"Is that what you want?" He tugs on my chin, forcing my lips to part.

"Maybe," I say as the doors behind him open.

"You let me know when you're sure." He steps back, leaving me disappointed as he takes my hand from the railing.

As soon as I step out of the elevator with him, I'm

confronted with exactly how much money he has. His place is ginormous with two full walls of window that overlook the rest of the buildings in the area and the sound, which I never realized is only blocks away. After releasing me, he walks across the open floor and tosses his bag on a sleek black couch that could seat the entire Brady bunch along with a few dozen more kids.

"Are scrambled eggs okay?" he asks as I slowly walk behind him toward the open kitchen with black cabinets, pure white countertops, and top-of-the-line stainless steel appliances.

"Sounds good." I keep walking toward the windows and look out. "I could never live up here. I'd feel like I lived in a fish tank and people were watching me all the time."

"That's why the windows can do this," he says and suddenly the windows seem to fill with smoke, blocking out the view.

"That's very fancy." I look at him over my shoulder so I can watch him laugh.

"A little too fancy. It took me a month to figure out how to use them," he replies as I walk to the large dining table and run my hand over the wood surface that looks like someone split a tree in half then glazed it, with the natural pits and grooves filled with some kind of gold flecks. Even the outer edge of bark is glazed over. "You like it?"

"It's very pretty. Where did you get it?" It looks custom made for the space and is big enough to sit at least twelve people or more if you added a few more chairs.

"I made it."

I lift my eyes off the table and meet his gaze. "You made this?"

He shrugs. "It's a hobby of mine."

Isn't he just full of surprises?

Then again, he's been surprising me since the moment we met. "Where did you get the wood?"

"I have a piece of land and a small cabin just outside the city," he explains, moving around in the kitchen while I walk around the table, inspecting it more closely. "I like to spend time there when I need to disconnect. There's no Internet and barely cell service, so I hike and look for fallen trees."

"Where did you learn to do woodworking?"

"My dad is a carpenter. I used to spend my summers helping him make custom pieces for people's homes. I hated it, but I guess it's still in my blood."

I laugh. "Yeah, I guess. I bet people would pay lots of money for a table like this."

"Maybe," he agrees as I take a seat on one of the barstools surrounding the outer edge of the kitchen island. "I don't sell the stuff I've made, and it takes me a while to finish anything, since I don't get away as much as I'd like. That table took me a little over a year to create."

"Is it the only thing you've made?"

"No. I made a coffee table for my mom, which she took the legs off of and hung on the wall." He grins, and I can't help but grin back. "Besides that, I've made a couple other things, but like I said, I don't have a lot of free time." He fills two cups with coffee out of a pot, handing one to me before going to the fridge and coming back with creamer.

"It must be tiring being the owner of a company, with so many people depending on you."

"It is, but I built IMG from the ground up and want it to be successful. It's like my baby, and I know if I put in the time now, later on down the road, it will take care of me."

"That's a good way to look at it," I say as he pulls a plate out of a drawer under the stove and piles it with fluffy-looking scrambled eggs.

I take it when he hands it over to me. "Ketchup or salsa?"

"Ketchup." I set the plate down, my stomach growling at the smell. A moment later, he comes back with the ketchup and a fork, handing me both. I add a large glob to the side of my plate then wait for him to bring his around. Once he's seated, I dig in, dipping the eggs in ketchup before I take a bite, almost moaning. I didn't notice him putting in cheese or spices, but it's delicious.

"Good?"

I turn and nod. "So good, thank you."

He grabs my knee, squeezing it, the small gesture giving me comfort and turning me on all at the same time. Honestly, there isn't much about him that doesn't turn me on, and the more I learn about him, the more

I like. He might have more money than one person could spend in a lifetime, but he's not your typical rich asshole. Or maybe he is and he just hasn't shown that side of himself to me. "So tell me about your family. Do they live in Washington?"

Darn, I should have been prepared for that question. The normal question you ask someone when you're getting to know them. The kind of question I dread, because I don't like people to feel sorry for me, and no matter how much I sugarcoat my past, that's exactly what happens. "As you know my brother lives here." I go with being evasive, hoping he'll read between the lines and let it go.

"And your parents?"

"They aren't around." I take another bite, feeling his eyes on me as I chew.

His hand lands back on my knee, and he holds it there, not saying anything, just waiting for me to look at him. When I do, his voice is soft as he asks, "Not around, as in they don't live here, or not around at all?"

"My dad passed when I was fifteen. My mom passed away two years later."

"Dakota—"

"Please don't," I say quietly, covering his hand with mine. "I don't want you to feel sorry for me."

"I don't feel sorry for you, Dakota. I just want to understand."

"My mom survived the car accident that killed my dad then she got addicted to pain medication and killed herself."

"So, you and Jamie…?"

"So me and Jamie wound up living in foster care. Thankfully, we found a family who took us both in, so things weren't as bad for us as they could have been if we'd been separated."

"Jesus."

"It could have been worse." I shrug, turning away from him, and begin moving my food from one side of my plate to the other.

"Don't do that." He squeezes my leg.

"Do what?" I turn to lock eyes with him.

"Try to play it off like that shit didn't mark you. Like you're hard as stone and nothing can hurt you." I rub my lips together while staring into his eyes. "It's okay to let your guard down and be vulnerable around me."

Is it? I mean, our relationship so far has been built on lies and a hefty amount of lust. It's not exactly the solid foundation you need in order to trust someone.

"Maybe one day I'll get to a place with you where I feel comfortable letting you see all the ugly parts of me," I say, wanting to be honest. "But right now, I'm not there."

"I get that." He lifts his hand and his fingers softly touch my cheek. "I just want you to know I'm here if you want to talk."

"I've dealt with my past, Braxton. I don't need a counselor or a therapist."

"I'm sure you don't but I would like to be your friend."

"None of my friends have seen me naked."

His lips twitch. "A different kind of friend then."

"Right." My own lips quirk into a smile then his wrist starts to flash, gaining his attention.

"Shit, I gotta take this call."

"That's okay," I say, catching a glimpse of the time. "I should go down to my place and get ready for work."

"I'm gonna assume there is no way I can convince you to hang out here in my bed all day."

I laugh, tossing my head back, and when my hilarity dies down, I find him watching me closely. "What?"

"Nothing, I just like hearing you laugh," he says softly, leaning in to touch his lips to my forehead. "Send me a message when you get down to your place."

"I'm just going downstairs. I doubt anyone is going to kidnap me."

"Just send me a text," he insists.

I give in with a sigh that makes him smile and stand. He takes my hand and walks me to the elevator, even though it's only across the room. When the doors open, I lift up on my tiptoes and kiss his cheek. "Have a good day at work."

"You too." He squeezes my waist then lets me go.

I step into the elevator and lean against the wall as the doors close, expecting him to come in and ravish me. But then I have to tell myself I'm not disappointed when that doesn't happen. I watch the numbers drop as I head to my place and wonder if it's too late to go back and tell him I'd like nothing more than to spend the day in his bed. But as much as I want that, I want my job. I want independence and a life I've built for myself.

I LOOK UP from my computer when someone clears their throat and smiles. "Hey, Mat."

"Mike." He points his thumb at his chest. "I'm Mike." Darn, I should be able to tell the two men I work with apart, but honestly, they look almost identical, both with brown wavy hair that's messily styled, both tan, and both attractive in that wholesome kind of way.

"Sorry." I smile sheepishly.

"It's okay. It happens." He shrugs, tucking his hands into the front pocket of his slacks. "I just wanted to come over and tell you that I really liked your show today. We all did." He looks around then leans into me. "Kathy is cool, but she's not really open to new ideas."

"I kind of got that." I laugh softly. During my entire show this afternoon she was watching me with a scowl and a whole lot of headshakes because I wasn't following her notes completely. Instead I was doing what I felt would draw in customers, and I think it worked since I sold out of the product I was presenting.

His eyes drop to my mouth, and he clears his throat before meeting my gaze once more. "A few of us are getting together after work tonight for a drink across the street at the Gull. It would be cool if you'd join us."

"I'd like that."

"Awesome, I'll see you there."

"Yeah, see you there," I agree, and he smiles before he turns and walks away. I glance down at my phone, wondering if I should send Braxton a message, then get annoyed with myself for even thinking about checking in with him. He's not my boyfriend; I don't need to let him know what I'm doing. Besides, I'm just going out for one drink. I can still meet him for dinner afterward. With that last thought, I get back to work, trying to incorporate Kathy's ideas with some of my own for the next time I'm scheduled to be on air which isn't easy to do, but I'm determined.

I yawn for the second time and glance at the clock on my computer, realizing then that I've been working for almost four hours straight. I rub my eyes then pick up my can of Coke to take a sip, finding it empty. Since it's about time for me to leave for the day, I shut down my computer then sigh when my desk phone rings. "Dakota Newton's desk," I answer after putting it to my ear.

"Dakota, please come to my office," Kathy's voice greets me, and then before I can even say "sure," the line goes dead. I inwardly groan and slip back on my black heels I kicked off under my desk and stand. I rub my hands down the front of my gray slacks and straighten my top before I head across the office, catching a few curious looks as I go.

When I reach Kathy's door, I knock twice, waiting for her to call for me to come in before I push the door open. I find her sitting behind her desk with a beautiful woman maybe a couple years older than me, sitting across from her. Both of them smile, but I can't tell if their smiles are genuine or not.

"Dakota, I'd like you to meet my niece Hanna. Hanna, this is Dakota."

Hanna, the Hanna Braxton dated, the Hanna he still works with. My stomach drops.

"Hi, Dakota." Hanna stands, and I instinctively hold out my hand toward her. She takes it, giving it a squeeze, then tips her head to the side. "You're even prettier in real life than you are on TV."

"Thank you." I say softly thinking she's pretty too, actually gorgeous with long blonde hair that is perfectly styled with the top pulled away from her face, making her bright blue eyes and pixie like features stand out. She's the kind of woman who would look perfect on the arm of a man like Braxton. Jealousy curls in the pit of my stomach on that thought, and I despise the emotion immediately.

"Hanna came down here today to talk to me about moving you upstairs," Kathy says, and my attention goes to her as Hanna releases the hold she has on me. "Apparently Braxton is insistent."

The feeling of jealousy in the pit of my stomach is replaced with annoyance at Braxton. We talked about this last night, and I thought I got through to him and that he was respecting me and my choice. I guess not. "I don't want to move."

"Braxton mentioned that," Hanna replies, and I focus on her. "But he showed Chris who is the head of marketing some of your show ideas, and Chris agreed with him. Your style is edgy, modern, and he thinks you could add a lot to our marketing team." She smiles, and I look over at Kathy, noting she looks anything but happy. "Chris would really like the chance to talk to you."

"That's very nice, and I don't want to seem unappreciative, but I really want to stay where I am," I say, praying Kathy doesn't think I've gone behind her back.

"I totally get it," Hanna tells me, taking a seat once more. "Let me know if and when you change your mind and I'll pass it along."

"Okay," I agree, feeling stuck—something I loathe. I don't want to make anyone mad, especially the person who took a chance on me in offering me a job in the first place. I also have no desire to work in marketing, this job is my dream job, I just hope I can prove to Kathy that I can bring something new and fresh while blending the old with the new.

"Now that you've officially tried to steal one of my employees, I think this meeting can be over," Kathy says, and Hanna laughs.

I force a grin in Kathy's direction. "I won't be that easy to get rid of."

"I'm thinking it might not be your choice."

Her words send a chill down my spine. A part of me knows she's right. It might not be my choice. I've danced with the devil, and now he's playing with my life. I want to resent him for stepping in and taking over even after I told him not to, but I'm not even sure he would understand. He's used to always getting his way, and I'm sure he thinks I'll eventually give in. I just don't understand why he's so insistent on me moving.

"It was so nice to meet you, Dakota. We should get a drink sometime," Hanna says, catching me off guard with the sincerity in her tone.

I really don't want to like her. But I can't help it. There is something about her that seems sweet. I just wonder if she would be so nice if she knew about Braxton and my current relationship.

I drag in a breath and smile at her putting the jealousy I feel aside. "I'd like that." I need friends here, and Braxton says their relationship is nothing but professional, maybe that's the truth and they are just friends. I guess only time will tell.

"I'll get your number from my aunt," she says, and I nod once then look at Kathy, catching her lift her chin ever so slightly toward the door, signaling me to leave.

"I look forward to that," I tell her then turn back to Kathy. "I'm going to head out. I'll see you tomorrow."

"Have a good evening, Dakota."

"You too." I turn on my heel and head out the door, back to being seriously annoyed with Braxton once again for his highhandedness.

Chapter 8

DAKOTA

I FEEL MY cell phone buzz in the back pocket of my jeans, and I don't even bother checking to see who it is. Braxton has been calling and messaging for the last hour and a half. I messaged him back after the first text, letting him know I was getting a drink with a few of my coworkers but would be at his place for dinner and conversation about him sending Hanna down to talk to Kathy and me.

Unsurprisingly, he sent a message immediately asking where I was having a drink, who I was having a drink with, and informing me that we didn't need to talk about Kathy or Hanna. I didn't bother disagreeing with him, since I want him to see my face when I reinforce my point.

When someone laughs loudly, I come out of my head

and look around the table, finding everyone cracking up; about what, I'm not sure. I've always been a little awkward when getting to know new people. I have a tendency to watch and listen before I let people in—a trait that makes people think I'm a bitch when I'm not.

Tonight, hasn't been any different. I don't know where I fit in. They've all been working together for a while. They have built friendships, have inside jokes, and are all alike in a way that makes me feel like an outsider.

"I think I'm going to call it a night," I say, and all eyes come to me.

"It's still early," my coworker Samantha replies, glancing at her watch. "Don't you want to at least finish your drink?"

I look at my second beer, which I only took a couple sips of, and shake my head. "I really should get home, I need to eat dinner and I want to get some sleep so that I'm ready for my show tomorrow."

"Don't overthink the shit Kathy says," Mat tells me with a shake of his head. "I've been working here for three years, and she's never liked any of my ideas, which sucks. But at the end of the day, it doesn't really matter. She doesn't have the final say, what matters are ratings and sales."

"Really?" That surprises me.

"Yeah, and the bigwigs know she's stuck in the past, but since her niece is sleeping with the CEO, it doesn't matter."

My stomach turns. Still, I manage to ask, "What do

you mean?”

I know Braxton said that he and Hanna are not together and haven’t been intimate, but could they be sleeping together? I didn’t think Troy was cheating on me. I didn’t have a clue until I saw photos.

“Mr. Adams and his assistant Hanna have been together forever. I wouldn’t be surprised if there are wedding bells at some point soon.”

“I would be,” a deep voice says from behind me, making me jump while Mat’s face pales.

Knowing who just arrived, I turn on my stool and glare up at the handsome guy who looks ready to pick me up and drag me out of here.

“Dakota.”

“Braxton,” I say, and his eyes narrow. “What are you doing here?”

“I’ve been calling you,” he replies, and I hear a gasp come from behind me. “You’re not picking up your phone.”

“I’m with friends.”

“I see that.” He looks around the table, and I have no doubt everyone is wondering what the hell is going on, how I know the CEO of IMG, and why he would be calling me. No doubt, they are coming up with a million different scenarios, and I’m sure that most of them would be correct. “Dinner is ready at my place.”

So much for keeping things between us on the low. “You are unbelievable.”

“So you’ve said.” His eyes lock with mine. “Are you ready to go or would you like to have a conversation here?"

"I hate you," I hiss just loud enough for him to hear as I stand, and then I turn to face the table, grabbing my bag. "I'm sorry, guys. I'll see you all tomorrow."

"Yeah… sure," Chris and Mat say in unison while the rest of the table of women stare at me in disbelief, their eyes ping-ponging back and forth between Braxton to me.

"Night." I turn and stomp past Braxton, wondering exactly what I would have to do to hurt him without hurting myself, because I swear to God the minute I get outside, I'm going to kick his ass for what he just did. Once again, he ignored me and what I wanted so he could get his way.

"Dakota." He tries to take my hand when I push out of the bar, but I jerk away, not wanting everyone I can feel watching from the windows of the bar to see me lose my mind.

I march swiftly down the block then hurry across the street, glancing at Braxton out the corner of my eye. He looks like he doesn't have a care in the world; then again, I guess he doesn't. His coworkers are not going to think he got his job by sleeping with the boss and that he's possibly a home-wrecker. "Might I ask where we're going?" he prompts when we reach the elevator in our building and step inside.

"To your place, so I can kill you without anyone watching," I bite out, getting even more pissed when his lips twitch. "This isn't funny, Braxton. I'm so mad at you right now."

"I know." He turns to face me after waving his watch across the front screen of the elevator, causing the doors to close.

"Why would you do that? Why would you show up when I told you just last night that I want to keep whatever this is quiet?"

"Dakota, I own this building, and this morning you made a show of leaving the gym with me. You don't think some of my employees witnessed that?"

Shit, I didn't even think about that. Why didn't I think about that? Oh right, because normal people don't own buildings. Normal people own houses or condos. I cross my arms over my chest and continue to glare at him.

"I'm sure the people who saw us leave the gym together have already started to spread rumors about you and me and what our relationship might be. You're not my dirty little secret, and I refuse to have anyone believe you are."

"It should have been my choice, Braxton." I shove a hand against his chest, and he captures it, holding it over his heart. "I really don't like you."

"That's okay. I like you enough for the two of us." He captures my other wrist when I try to push him away then begin to pant when he maneuvers my hands behind my back, bringing us chest-to-chest and face-to-face. "You make me crazy."

"Then we're even," I hiss, pushing up on my tiptoes—something I realize was the wrong move as his breath brushes my lips. "Let me go."

"Never."

"Braxton." I start to panic as desire begins to swirl in my stomach.

"Dakota." I swallow and drop my eyes to his mouth.

"Tell me you want it, tell me to kiss you."

I lick my lips then whisper, "Kiss me, Braxton."

His mouth crashes down on mine and he kisses me, forcing his tongue between my lips as he drags me out of the elevator, my bag slipping off my shoulder. He catches it, and I get one of my hands free, using it to pull his shirt out of his slacks so I can run my hand up over his abs. He uses his free hand to toss my bag away before he tangles his fingers in my hair at the back of my head, keeping me right where he wants me.

"Braxton," I breathe when he lets my mouth go to kiss down my neck.

"Don't deny me, Dakota." He sounds desperate as he lets go of my other wrist so he can slide his hand under my shirt to the waistband of my pants. "I need you." He moves around my waist and he flicks open the button of my grey slacks before sliding his hand into my panties, his fingers finding my clit, making my knees weak as he rolls over it.

I latch onto his shoulder, digging my nails in as he turns us and walks me backward, his mouth coming back to mine while I work at getting his shirt unbuttoned.

Obviously fed up with us fumbling our way to his bed, he scoops me up and carries me across the room to a wall of smoky glass doors. He slides them open one-handed and takes me to the side of the bed, dropping me to my feet at the side.

"Clothes off." He steps back and slips out of his shirt before working his belt buckle loose. I watch him with fascination, his body like a work of art that needs to be appreciated. "Dakota," he growls, making me jump. "Take your clothes off if you don't want me to shred them."

I lick my lips and slip off my flats before I slowly pull my top over my head. When he has nothing on but his pants, I push my grey slacks down my thighs.

"Fuck, I can see how wet you are." His eyes devour me from head to toe as I stand before him in nothing but my panties and a bra, breathing heavy. I wait for him to touch me, my skin already on fire with anticipation. He steps toward me, his hand balling into a fist like he's not sure where to start, where to touch me first.

I put my hands behind my back and unclasp my bra, letting it fall from my shoulders. His eyes darken and his jaw tics as the material lands on the floor. I don't hesitate to slip off my panties, and I'm so wet the cool air makes me shiver.

"Now what?" I question.

"I'm trying to figure that out." He reaches for me, his finger skimming the tip of my nipple, and it tightens. "I don't know where to start. I don't know if I want to eat you first or bend you over the bed and fuck you until you scream my name."

I don't tell him I'll be happy either way, but judging by the way his lips curve up ever so slightly, he knows what I'm thinking. I hold my breath as he walks around me and moan when he cups my breast from behind, lowering his mouth to my shoulder. My head tips to the side, giving him access to my neck as one of his hands travels slowly down my stomach to between my legs.

The first touch of his fingers makes my head fall back and my eyes slide closed. He nips my earlobe as his fingers slide past my clit to fill me, and I start to open my legs wider, to give him more room, but his teeth sink into my flesh in a silent demand not to move. I grab hold of his forearm, willing myself to hold strong. The pleasure builds, threatening to bring me to my knees as his fingers thrust into me slowly and his thumb rolls over my clit.

Just as I'm about to fall over the edge, he moves me around to face the bed and bends me over. My core tightens right before I cry out in frustration when he removes his fingers from me, and then I cry out for a different reason when he drops to his knees and his mouth latches onto my clit from behind. His fingers dig into my hips to hold me in place as he devours me like he's starving, his tongue, teeth, and lips sending me closer to the edge.

My body shakes and my toes try to find purchase against the wood floor as my head thrashes from side to side. When his thumb presses against my entrance, I fall over the cliff, shouting his name. Stars fill my vision, my body feels light as a feather, and my skin tingles from my hips to my toes. Just as I'm starting to come back to myself, his body covers mine and he enters me without warning in one smooth thrust.

The head of his cock bumps my cervix, and I feel him throb inside me, seeming to take up every inch of space. Wanting more of him, *needing* more of him, I lift up on my hands and push back against him, listening to him groan. He wraps his hand around my hair when I toss my head back, and then he pulls me up, angling my head so he can cover my mouth with his. His mouth is hungry, desperate, and branding as he kisses me, and in that moment, I know I'm already his.

He fucks me harder and harder until I'm once again stumbling over the edge of pleasure, only this time he falls with me, locking his hips against mine after one final thrust. We both tumble forward onto the bed, his body heavy on top of mine and our breathing erratic as we soak up the last pulse of pleasure.

When he rolls away, I miss his weight but then relish the feel of his skin against mine as he drapes me across his chest and once more tangles his fingers into my hair. I rest my forehead in the crook of his neck and wrap my hand around his side, feeling sated and sleepy.

"Are you okay?" His voice is gruff but warm, and I tip my head back to meet his gaze.

"Yeah, are you?"

"Better, now that I've had you again." He smiles when I smack his chest. "What? I missed you."

"You missed the vagina."

His eyes lock with mine, looking deadly serious. "No, I missed *you*."

I chew on my bottom lip then swallow. I want to tell him that I missed him too, that I missed connecting with him like we just did, even if we only shared that for one night, but I manage to keep my mouth shut.

He sighs then smooths a finger across my forehead to behind my ear. "I can wait."

I somehow doubt that. Instead of pointing out his behavior, I rest my head back against his chest, and then my stomach growls when I smell something delicious. It reminds me that I didn't eat anything but a package of mixed nuts at lunch today, because I was anxious to get back to work so I could try to impress Kathy with some new ideas for tomorrows show. "I'm starving."

"You wouldn't be so hungry if you'd just come here when you were supposed to."

"I didn't give you a time when I would be here," I remind him, lifting my head off his chest to narrow my eyes on him. "And I went out, because I wanted to try to get to know the people I work with, since I do have to work with them and wouldn't mind having some friends."

"I'm your friend."

If I'm not wrong, there is a little bit of jealousy in his tone, like I couldn't possibly want to be friends with anyone else when I've got him.

"You're also the CEO of IMG. I can't talk crap about my job or your company to you."

"Why not?" he asks, kissing me swiftly before rolling me off him and getting out of bed.

I blink at the sudden change of position, unsure if he's serious, and when I see he is, I just shake my head, not even attempting to help him understand. I get up and start to search for my clothes but stop when he hands me a T-shirt. I put it on over my head, and it hits me midthigh, long enough that I don't need to worry about pants.

"Let's feed you," he says, walking out of the bedroom, wearing nothing but his boxers, and I follow him, glaring at his back as I hop into my panties.

"Let's talk about you sending Hanna down to talk to Kathy."

"That was not me; that was all Chris. He saw your work," he replies over his shoulder as he walks toward the kitchen.

"You showed Chris my work."

He smiles. "I showed him your work, and he agreed with me and thought we should send Hanna down to try to convince you to meet with him." He disappears as he bends at the waist, and then a moment later, he comes up with a pan covered with foil, placing it on the counter.

"You should know that didn't convince me. All it did was make me mad."

"I got that from your message." He sighs, getting out two plates, and then he goes to the fridge, grabbing two bowls filled with salad.

"Do you want help?" I might be annoyed, but I

don't want to be rude.

"You can pick a bottle of wine," he says then lifts his chin in the direction of the dining table. "I have a wine room. You'll see it now that you know you're looking for it."

"A wine room?" I repeat in disbelief.

"A wine room." He grins.

"You have too much money." I step away from the kitchen, hearing him laugh as I head around the corner, seeing a large wood-framed door with tinted glass. I walk toward it and the light turns on, allowing the bottles of wine inside to be seen. I open the door and step into the room, overwhelmed while looking around at the shelves lining the walls. I don't even know what kind of wine goes with what foods—not that it would help if I did, since I don't know what we're eating.

Grabbing one of the bottles, I take it with me out of the room toward the kitchen but stop when a large painting catches my attention. I tip my head one way then the other, trying to understand what I'm looking at. I'm not sure, but it kind of looks like a woman sitting naked on a toilet, but that would be weird.

"Sweetheart, don't even bother trying to figure out what it is," Braxton says, and I look over to find him leaning his shoulder against the wall, watching me.

"Is it a woman on the toilet?"

"It could be." He shrugs, pushing off the wall to step toward me then takes the bottle of wine before grasping my hand. "Are you ready to eat?"

"Why do you have a painting of a woman on a toilet

in your dining room?" I ask when he pulls out a stool in a silent demand for me to sit, so I do.

"My mom painted it. She took an art class a few years ago and convinced herself that she's now an artist," he says, leaving me on the opposite side of the counter as he walks back around into the kitchen, still speaking. "She gave me that painting as a housewarming gift, and then she hung it. I don't have the heart to take it or the other pieces she's hung down."

He stops to inspects the bottle of wine I chose, and I blurt, "I don't know anything about wine."

"You might not, but you chose well. This exact bottle of Penfolds Grange Hermitage was auctioned off a couple years ago for close to fifty grand."

My jaw drops. "You're joking."

"Nope," he says as he places some kind of apparatus onto the top of the bottle and starts to press the button.

I shoot up out of my chair when he turns it on and climb up on the island. "What are you doing?"

"Opening the wine." He eyes me where I'm now balanced on top of the counter, reaching toward him.

"You can't open that." I try to grab it, but I'm too far away.

"Why not?"

"Because you just said it cost fifty thousand dollars. You don't ingest something that cost fifty thousand dollars."

"Dakota, it's wine. It's meant to be enjoyed."

"Well, my wine pallet isn't refined enough to enjoy it, so give it to someone who at least loves wine enough to know what kind of wine goes best with meat or noodles."

"You enjoy wine." He presses the button, and the contraption makes a whirring sound that sends my heart into my stomach.

"I can't believe you're opening it," I groan, falling face-forward onto the counter. "That's more than what most people make in a year and enough money to put a kid through college."

"It's also just wine," he says, and I lift my head to glare at him. "If it makes you feel better, I didn't buy it. It was a gift."

"No, that does not make me feel better. And who gives gifts like that?"

"People with too much money," he replies, smiling, and I nod, because he's right. Only people with way too much money would give someone a bottle of wine that costs so much. "Do you want to sit on the counter to eat or on the stool?" he asks, and I sigh, getting down.

Instead of taking a seat, I walk around into the kitchen and help him get things together, placing our salads and forks on the island while he pours the wine and dishes out some kind of chicken with a creamy-looking sauce over wild rice. After everything is done, we both take a seat, and I pick up my wineglass to inspect it for the sparkle of magic that must be hidden in the glass.

"Let's toast," he says, and I swivel his way, meeting his warm gaze.

"What are we toasting to?"

"The unexpected but appreciated." He taps his glass against mine then takes a sip. I follow suit, rolling the warm liquid around in my mouth, really trying to comprehend why it cost so much. I don't get it; it tastes like my favorite red that I get from the grocery store for seven bucks, and if I'm honest… my grocery store wine tastes better.

"What do you think?"

"I think whoever paid for this should ask for their money back. I don't have magical powers, and I don't think you do either."

He laughs, and my chest warms. I really don't know how I can go from being so angry at him to just enjoying his presence. I'm totally falling for him, even though he's a liar, overbearing, and probably the completely wrong man for me.

"Dig in before your food is cold. I called my mom for this recipe, and she'll be disappointed if you don't like it."

I pick up my fork and take a bite of tender chicken, salty capers, zesty lemon, and perfectly cooked rice. After I chew and swallow, I lock eyes with him. "You can tell your mom it's delicious."

"She didn't cook it."

I grin. "Are you digging for a compliment?"

"Absolutely, I'm trying to impress you."

"You don't have to try too hard," I say then add, "When you're not annoying me, I actually really do like you."

"That's good to know." His eyes search mine like he's trying to see into my soul, only I have no idea what he's looking for. "So how was work today?"

"Work." I shrug, taking another bite off my plate, unwilling to talk to him about it—not with him being my boss's boss's boss's boss.

"You know you can talk to me about work—as a friend, not the CEO—right?"

"Like I can talk to you about other things and have you respect what I say without going behind my back?"

"I haven't gone behind your back."

I guess he hasn't. He's put it all out there with everyone, including now my coworkers, who I'm sure will have questions for me tomorrow. "All I'm saying is I would like to keep a little bit of separation between what is happening between you and me and work. I don't want to make things even more complicated."

"So what happens with work when you're ready to admit you're mine?"

"Yours?"

"Mine," he confirms with a hungry look. "I'm not going to pretend we aren't together, Dakota, just to make other people who don't mean shit to me feel better."

"Do you always have to be so aggressive?"

"I think you know the answer to that." Judging by the way my body is feeling, I guess I do.

"Fine, work was good. Hanna is very nice, and I thought I was making progress with the people I work with, but now I'm sure they're wondering why you showed up at the bar and what's going on between us. I'm also nervous about what will happen when that news gets back to Kathy, because it will. Maybe not tomorrow, but it will. I do believe you when you say nothing is going on between you and your assistant, but I think Kathy is convinced otherwise, and so is everyone else."

"Fuck what everyone else thinks."

"That's easy for you to say."

"It's not complicated, Dakota," he says, sounding pissed, which annoys me. He has nothing to be mad about. I didn't lie to him or come in and disrupt his life.

"You have a penis, Braxton, and you're sitting upstairs in your private office bossing everyone around. No one would dare make it seem like you're in the wrong."

"If anyone ever made you feel uncomfortable, I'd deal with them."

I groan, tossing my head back. "That right there is exactly what I'm talking about! You can't just come in and piss all over the place or throw the fact that you're the boss around to get your way."

"I have to disagree with you on that."

"This is pointless." I set down my fork and let out a deep breath, back to being frustrated. It's like talking to a brick wall trying to make him see things from my point of view.

"I'm sorry." He sets down his own fork and turns his stool toward me before swiveling me around to face him. Once he has my knees trapped between his, he takes my hands.

"Sorry for what?" I mean, let's be honest; there is a whole lot for him to apologize for, and I really doubt he thinks he's done anything wrong.

"For upsetting you."

"You piss me off, Braxton. You don't upset me."

"Is there a difference?" he asks, sounding curious.

"Yes, being upset is when you are disappointed or unhappy. Pissed is when you are just plain mad, and *you* make me angry to the point of seeing red. You're not just some regular guy; you're the CEO of the company I work for, which means you have the upper hand. And when it comes to my career, I need to know my success is my own, and I don't want anyone to think I've gotten where I am because I'm sleeping with the boss."

"I didn't know you when you got the job with IMG, Dakota. You did that all on your own."

"I know, but no one will care about that when they find out about us."

His eyes stay locked on mine, and I see the wheels in his head turning, trying to figure out how to get his way while making me believe I got mine. "I don't want to lie to you again, and me telling you that I'm sorry people know there is something going on between us would be a lie."

I drop my eyes from his, unsure how to respond. Part of me is happy he doesn't want to hide me away like a dirty secret. Another part of me is mad I don't get a say in when people find out.

"Dakota." He squeezes my hands, but his cell phone rings, cutting off whatever he was going to say. He turns his wrist to check his watch. "Fuck, I'll be right back," he tells me before brushing his lips across the top of my head.

After he gets up, I turn back to my plate and ponder what I should do. It's honestly too late for me to worry about people finding out about us, especially after what happened tonight. And with him being who he is, it would only be a matter of time anyway. Not because he's the CEO, but because he is so overbearing and determined to make some kind of public claim on me.

I finish eating then drink the rest of my wine—and his—while waiting for him to come back. When that doesn't happen, I get up and take my plate around to the sink, rinsing it off before placing it in the dishwasher. Chewing my nail, I lean against the counter then say screw it, going in search of Braxton. I find him on the phone in what looks like his office, his back to me, his phone to his ear.

I shut the door before he sees me and wander back to the kitchen to pour myself another glass of wine. Maybe drinking it will give me what I need to impress Kathy. I go to the couch, grabbing my phone out of my purse, and then make myself comfortable and open the kindle app on my phone and get lost in someone else's complicated relationship.

"Baby," Braxton's deep voice whispers against my ear as he lifts me against his chest, and I automatically burrow into his warmth. "Are you awake?"

"Yeah." I try to pull myself out of the cocoon of sleep, but it's difficult between my early morning, the orgasms Braxton gave me, and the three glasses of wine I had tonight.

"So sweet." His lips touch my forehead right before I'm placed back down on a soft surface.

Then he settles in behind me, his fingers slide over my bare hip before a blanket is settled over me. "Sleep, sweet girl."

I turn to face him and burrow against his chest. "Just for a few minutes, and then I'll go home," I whisper back, feeling his lips lingering against my forehead before I'm captured by his warm scent and once more dragged under by sleep.

Chapter 9

DAKOTA

I WALK INTO the IMG building fifteen minutes late, cursing Braxton for taking advantage of me being in his bed this morning and using my body against me. Not that I didn't enjoy myself. I just didn't even think about the time or the fact that I had to be at work when he was giving me a good morning orgasm and I thought about it less when he told me that the phone call he got last night was from one of his contacts in New York and that he was going to be leaving for a few days.

I keep my head straight as I get on the elevator and don't even acknowledge my coworkers as I walk to my desk. Once I'm settled with my computer open in front of me, I start to bite my nails, anxiously awaiting the moment anyone comes over to question me about what happened last night.

After thirty minutes, my muscles begin to relax, and I pull up the courage to look around. Not one person is glancing in my direction with suspicious or judgmental looks. Really, it seems it's business as usual. I take a deep breath and let it out slowly. Maybe I worried for nothing about what my coworkers would think about Braxton coming to the bar last night. Maybe they don't care… or maybe they are too scared to confront me.

I start up my computer and open my schedule and the talk points I had been going over yesterday. Just as I'm about to send them over to Kathy for approval, an e-mail pops up on my screen and my heart pounds as I click it open.

From: Hanna Mathers
Subject: Request from Mr. Adams

Dakota,

Mr. Adams asked me to reach out to you in hopes you could help him choose a high school recipient to receive $50,000 toward their college education. I know this might be an odd request, but he's assured me that you would understand.

Please e-mail me back at your convenience with the contact information for who you've chosen, and I will take care of the rest.

All the best,

Hanna

"Oh my God." I cover my mouth with my shaking fingers and tears fill my eyes. I can't believe he is doing this, and I doubt he knows how much this gesture means to me. That money could change someone's life, especially a kid who is currently in the foster care system.

Most kids who grow up in the system don't even dare to dream of going to college, and those who do quickly realize how difficult it will be for them if they do get into a school. Knowing exactly what I'm going to do, I send Hanna a quick return e-mail to let her know I will be in contact then go online to look up Jamie's and my old caseworker. After tracking her down, I send her an e-mail with my phone number and ask her to call me when she has a few minutes to talk.

With that done, I forward my ideas to Kathy, not really caring if she likes them or not. There isn't much that could put a damper on my mood right now. A message pops up a minute later from Kathy with the entire team attached, asking all of us to meet her in one of the conference rooms upstairs.

I head to the elevator, and my forgotten anxiety returns when Samantha smiles at me with a knowing look in her eyes. Not wanting her to think she has something over me, I press the up arrow while asking, "Did you guys have fun last night?"

She shrugs. "I took off not long after you left with—" She pauses, glancing around. "—Mr. Adams. I didn't know who he was until Mat said he's the CEO of IMG."

"Yep, he's the head honcho," I say like an idiot, and she laughs.

"Do you guys know what this is about?" Chris asks, joining us just when the elevator doors open and we all step on together.

"No idea," I reply, taking a step back as Chris holds the door open for more people to get on with us. Once the doors close, everyone starts asking each other what this meeting could be about, and the more they talk, the curiouser I become. The way they are making it sound, this isn't a normal occurrence.

When we get upstairs, we file into the conference room and are asked to sit wherever we find our names. That's when I notice small boxes placed around the table, the same type of small box my watch came in. The watch I haven't worn since Braxton forced it on me.

"Hello, everyone." Kathy stands and moves to the head of the table. "I asked you all here this morning to talk to you about a product IMG will be launching in a few short months. If you would all be so kind as to open the boxes placed in front of you."

She pauses, and everyone does as asked with abandon, while I reluctantly join in. With the top off, I glare at the blinking red light, absently hearing everyone else ooh and ahh over the new watch they just received.

"The watch each of you are now holding is part of our new lifestyle line. This watch is designed to connect to all your current apps and devices along with all IMG exclusive products without you having to do anything but tap it to whatever you are connecting it to, which will make it more user-friendly with our older customers and even those millennials who don't want to waste their time programing another device." She smiles, holding up her wrist to show off her watch. "The goal is that you will never have to carry your phone, credit card, or even your keys again. Everything you need will be available to you twenty-four hours a day, seven days a week, right from your wrist."

Again, everyone oohs and ahhs while fastening the watch to their wrist. This time, I don't follow along I set the box down and turn it away from me as Kathy continues.

"This product was originally only given to the members of the board to test out, but Mr. Adams asked that I allow the team that will be selling it to experience the watch firsthand. He wants you to believe in it as much as he does." She smiles, glancing around the room. "I can tell you from personal experience that this little watch has made my life easier, and I hope you all feel the same. I want you to wear it and give your honest feedback over the next few months. If you find anything you don't like, please let me know so I can pass it along."

I smile along with everyone else then look over to my side when my shoulder is nudged by Samantha, who is now proudly wearing her new tracking device.

"Aren't you going to put yours on?" she asks, nodding to my box.

I don't want to. I *really* don't want to, because I have a feeling Braxton has manipulated this entire scenario. He knows I haven't worn the watch since he forced it on me, and by doing this, I no longer have a choice when it comes to wearing it.

"Yeah." I shake my head like I just had a moment of ditsy forgetfulness. "I just got caught up in what Kathy was saying." I pick up my box and take out the watch, the blinking light taunting me as I wrap it around my wrist. Once I have it secure, I pull the sleeve of my blouse down over it. I might be forced to wear it all the time, but that doesn't mean I have to take the time to charge it. If it dies, it dies; there is nothing he can do about that.

"You might have noticed there is no charging cable in your box," Kathy says, and I look at her, feeling my heart plummet. "This watch is charged by the sun, unlike some of our competitors', which allows you to never have to worry about plugging it in."

"Great," I groan, and everyone looks at me. "Sorry." I hold up my wrist. "I'm just so relieved I don't need to charge this beauty."

Kathy clears her throat, and everyone turns to focus on her once more. "I look forward to hearing from each of you, and as you know, my door is always open. Now." She motions toward the door. "Let's get back to work and sell, sell, sell."

I stand with everyone else, the weight on my wrist feeling heavier than ever before. I swear I'm going to kill Braxton for once again using his position to get his way.

"Are you okay?" Samantha asks as we wait for the elevator.

"Yeah, totally. Are you?" I ask automatically, glancing over when she laughs.

"You're a horrible liar. Has anyone ever told you that?" She grasps my wrist to pull my hand away from my mouth. Damn, I didn't even notice I was biting my nails. "My friend Mary back home always bites her nails when something is wrong or when she's worried. What's wrong?"

Knowing I should give her something, I sigh then lower my voice as we step out of the elevator and walk across the office toward our desks. "I'm a little nervous about what Kathy is going to say about the talk points I sent her this morning. She hasn't exactly been very open to anything I've given her so far."

"Every time I've seen you on air so far, you've been amazing, and like Mat said, Kathy doesn't have the final say, so I don't think you should worry too much about her opinion. Just do your best; that's all any of us can really do."

"You're right, thanks."

"Anytime. Also, I'm here if you ever need someone to bounce ideas off of. I know for me it helps my process."

"I'd really like that. We should exchange numbers and get together sometime," I say then shake my head. "Sorry. I don't mean to sound so desperate, but I could use a friend here."

"Well, you're in luck. I'm in the market for a friend." She laughs then asks, "Do you want to get lunch this afternoon? I was thinking of trying out that new chowder place a couple blocks over. I read a review that said they have the best sourdough bread bowls in the US. Something I doubt, since I grew up in San Francisco. Still, I want to try them out."

"I'm not sure what a sourdough bread bowl is, but I'd love to join you."

"If this place is any good, your mind is going to be blown." She says then looks at her new watch. "Wow, so cool. It just reminded me that I'm due on air in an hour." Her eyes widen. "Shit, I have to get to makeup." She starts to take off then turns back toward me, walking backward. "I should be done around one, but I'll let you know if I get done before then."

"Sounds good. And good luck."

"Thanks." She turns and calls over her shoulder, heading for hair and makeup on the opposite side of the room from me.

I go back to my desk and check over the list of the reports that were e-mailed to me this morning. After going through each one, I notice my numbers are right on point with some of the other people who have been on air here for years but vary depending on the state. I check to see if Kathy has e-mailed me back, and when I see she has, I open the e-mail and my heart sinks. Once more, she's dismissed the ideas I had on ways to promote the products on my schedule.

Not ready to give up, I go through some of the past

projects she's headed, finding they have performed well but not great by any standards. I would understand her being set on using her formula if it was working, but it hasn't been. By the time I'm done going over all the information I've found, my brain is tired and I'm confused and convinced that maybe it's me she doesn't like.

"I'm back," Samantha says, stopping at the edge of my desk, and I look up at her. "I'm just going to grab my purse. Want to meet me at the elevator?"

"Yes, I'll be right there." I start to shut down my computer, thinking maybe food will make me feel better, but stop when an e-mail from Sawyer Markel, my old social worker, pops up. My bad mood instantly lifts when I see she sent me her cell number along with a brief message asking how I have been and letting me know it will be easier if I call her. After I program her number into my phone, I meet Samantha, and I head out to lunch with my hopefully new friend.

"So what do you think?" Samantha asks as we finish up lunch.

"I'm not sure I'm a good judge. I was starving, so I think I could have eaten my own hand," I admit, and she smiles, looking at my empty plate before pulling off one more piece of her sourdough bowl and popping it in her mouth. "Did you enjoy it?"

"It was good, but there is nothing like having seafood while looking out at the bay. Have you ever heard of Fisherman's Wharf?"

"I went to San Francisco once with my ex and

he took me there, though we didn't have the clam chowder. We went to some fancy restaurant with his father. Honestly, I don't even remember the meal. I think I slept through most of it."

She cracks a smile then gets a faraway look in her eyes. "Every time I go back home to visit my family, I make them take me there to eat as soon as I land."

"What made you choose Seattle if your family is in California?" I know I could never be that far away from Jamie.

"I wanted to prove to myself and my family that I could survive on my own. So far, I'm doing okay, but I don't know if I will stay here after my contract is up with IMG. My sister just had a kid, and I feel like I'm missing out on all the fun aunt stuff." She pulls out her phone and shows me a photo of an adorable baby with chubby cheeks.

"He's cute."

"Right?" She looks at the photo herself then tucks it away in her pocket. "Do you have family here in Seattle?"

"My brother's here."

"That's cool. Are you two close?"

"Yeah, very." I smile. "He's annoying, but he's also my best friend."

"I have a brother, so I get it." She grins, and I grin back.

"Actually, he has a show this Friday and I promised him I'd show for a little while. Do you have plans?" I ask, hoping she says she doesn't.

"My only plans involved me lying on the couch in my pajamas, eating junk food, and watching reality TV, so no."

"Well, there won't be junk food but there will be alcohol, and the groupies who show up when he and his band perform are more entertaining than any reality TV show you might watch, so you're night will be the same minus the pajamas."

"Sounds like a good time to me," she says, checking her watch. "Darn, it's already time to get back. I'm going to use the restroom really quick."

"I'll wait here." Once she's gone, I pull out my cell and notice I have a couple messages from Braxton and one from Troy. I let out an annoyed breath as I read Troy's message explaining he didn't see the point of mailing my box like he said he would a week ago, because he will be in the city tomorrow evening and wants to meet up to give it to me. Even though I have no desire to see his face, I tell him that I can meet him at the coffee shop near my building.

I exit his message and go to Braxton's text next, chewing the inside of my cheek as I try not to smile as I read.

BRAXTON: I WISH I COULD HAVE TAKEN YOU ON THIS TRIP WITH ME. I THOUGHT ABOUT KIDNAPPING YOU MORE THAN ONCE BUT DIDN'T THINK IT WOULD GO OVER WELL. CALL ME WHEN YOU GET HOME TONIGHT, I SHOULD BE IN MY HOTEL BY THEN.

I shake my head. I don't know how I can be annoyed and enamored with him at the same time. I message him back, letting him know I will call but that he might not want me to, since I mostly want to yell at him about the watch I'm currently wearing. As soon as I press Send, he messages back.

BRAXTON: I LIKE WHEN YOU'RE ANGRY WITH ME. I LIKE IT MORE WHEN YOU LET ME HAVE MY WAY WITH YOU.

I message back, ignoring the way my spine tingles.

ME: I'M SERIOUS, BRAXTON. YOU REALLY NEED TO LEARN ABOUT BOUNDARIES.

Again, his response is immediate.

BRAXTON: WE DON'T HAVE BOUNDARIES BETWEEN US.

Gah, he really makes me want to scream. Instead of texting him back, I shove my phone into my bag then get up. I take Samantha's and my trash to the garbage across the room then wait for her near the front door, ignoring my watch as it seems to buzz nonstop, laughing to myself. He might have been able to force me to wear it, but he can't force me to use it, and I know that is really going to annoy him.

I sit in the middle of my bed with a smile on my face after hanging up the phone. Sawyer Markel was more than willing to help me find a kid who could use the college money and told me that she knew the perfect recipient, a young guy who had lost his mother to cancer but still has managed to get almost straight A's. He had a scholarship for Boulder University but still needed money to pay for room and board along with other necessities. After she told me about him I couldn't have agreed more with her choice. I send Hanna an email with Sawyer's information and explain the situation. Then with a smile still on my face I dial Braxton's number. Once the phone starts to ring, I set it down next to my laptop.

"Dakota," he answers, sounding tired. Not like he just woke up but just exhausted, like he's been going nonstop.

"Have you stopped going since you left here?" I ask him, concern filling my chest.

"I'm in bed now, I've had meetings since my flight touched down."

"I'm sorry," I say quietly.

"I'm all right… and better now that I hear your voice."

"Don't be sweet when I want to be mad at you."

"You don't have to be mad at me. You can just tell me how much you miss me so I can tell you how much I miss you. And how pissed I am that I'm not going to be back until Sunday."

"Sunday?" My heart sinks as I start to feel overwhelmed with disappointment.

"Sorry, baby, I had no idea this trip was even going to happen, but now that I'm here, I'm fitting in a few things I needed to take care of anyway."

"I guess it's part of the job, right?"

"Unfortunately," he agrees with a tired sigh. "I was planning on taking you to dinner this weekend."

I can't help but smile. "Were you planning on asking me to dinner or just telling me that we were going to dinner?" My phone lights up, so I click on the green button. A moment later, I see his gorgeous face.

"Did you have plans with someone else this weekend?" he asks as I pick up my phone so he can better see me.

"I actually had plans with my very attractive sugar daddy, but he had to run out of town on business," I say, and his lips curve up into a smile.

"Sorry you had to miss out on that."

"Me too, especially since he feeds me and allows me to drink very expensive wine."

"He sounds like a keeper."

I shrug, unsure he can see it. "I don't know. He's also overbearing and is always doing things to get his way that I don't always appreciate."

"Maybe he does those things to make sure you're safe. Sometimes us men want to protect the things that are most important to us."

"Maybe," I agree. "Then again, he might just be crazy, since we hardly know each other."

"I think you might be the thing making him crazy. He doesn't know what to do. You're the one thing in his life he can't fully control, and it's driving him mad."

"I think he's making *himself* insane," I grumble.

He chuckles. "So what are your plans for this week, now that you won't be doing me?"

I laugh then lie down on my bed, holding him up

over my face. "I'm going to Jamie's show on Friday, and Samantha is going to come with me."

"Samantha?"

I roll my eyes. "She's one of your employees."

"Sweetheart, I have a lot of employees. I don't know all of them by name."

"You should. They are all a part of your company. I watched a show once, and this CEO sends each and every one of his employees a handwritten card every year on their birthday."

"You want me to send each of my employees a birthday card?"

"It would be nice, and maybe give them a gift too," I say then frown. "Why are you laughing?"

"You're adorable."

"I wasn't trying to be adorable. I was trying to help you be a better boss."

"Most of my employees live in my building for free, have access to a gym and a swimming pool, and not to mention get great health and retirement benefits. I think I'm an okay boss."

Darn, he has a point. "Whatever."

His lips quirk. "It's okay to say I'm right."

"I still think a birthday card would be nice," I reply, refusing to give in, and he laughs, the sound making me strangely happy.

"So, you and Samantha are going to your brother's show. Any other plans this week?"

My stomach fills with worry. I don't know how that watch works or if he is still digitally attached to me, but if he is, he might know about me meeting up with Troy. Even though I have nothing to feel guilty about, guilt still fills the pit of my stomach along with a hefty dose of irritation.

"Are you still digitally stalking me?" I blurt.

His brows pull together. "Pardon? Digitally stalking you?"

"Are you connected to all my personal stuff with your watch—you know, my e-mail and texts and stuff?" When he doesn't answer right away but gets an almost panicked look in his eyes, I know he is. I also know he already knows about me meeting up with Troy and is fishing to see if I will tell him about it. "Are you going to answer me?"

"I'm not stalking you." His voice is placating, which only serves to piss me off even more.

"Do you know I'm meeting Troy tomorrow?" I ask, and his jaw tics, giving me my answer. "You know."

"I know," he confirms.

"Do you understand how violated that makes me feel?"

"Dakota—"

"No, Braxton, you need to get this, really get this. Unless I tell you something, it's none of your business."

"You're my business."

"Bye, Braxton." My thumb hovers over the red button on the screen.

"Do not hang up on me, Dakota," he growls, sending a chill down my spine.

"Or what?" I see the wheels in his head spinning.

He's on the other side of the country, literally. He can't just barge in, and even if he got on a plane, it would be hours before he was back here.

"Dakota, don't play games with me."

"Braxton, the only one playing games is you." I hang up and drop my phone to my side, and when it rings a second later, I turn it off. He has another think coming if he believes he can just go through my e-mails and texts without me having a reaction. Who the hell does that?

"A crazy man," I whisper, thinking I might be a little crazy myself, because even though I'm mad, I'm not as mad as I probably should be.

Chapter 10

DAKOTA

$\mathcal{I}$ SIT AT a small table in the back of the coffee shop with an iced coffee on the table in front of me, the condensation on the cup melting down onto the wooden surface, the drink forgotten since I sat down. All of my attention has been focused on the familiar-looking man across the room, the same man I saw the day I had brunch with Jamie, the same guy I thought I saw at the movies.

I don't want to assume he's somehow connected to Braxton, but my gut is screaming at me that he is. I narrow my eyes on him when he looks in my direction, and he frowns, making me question my own sanity.

"Dakota."

I look up at Troy, and he hesitates, like he's waiting for me to stand and greet him with a hug. There is no chance in hell I'm hugging him. I can barely even stand the sight of his still-handsome face. With a sigh, he takes a seat across from me, and I glance at the guy across the room to see his reaction to Troy's arrival, only he doesn't react at all. Okay, maybe I'm being paranoid.

"Do you know that guy?" Troy asks, gaining my attention.

"No." I pick up my coffee and take a huge gulp. Maybe I'm just on edge, because since I hung up on Braxton last night, I've been waiting for him to just show up or do something to let me know he's still around.

"Okay…" His brows pull together. "Well, you've been glaring at him since I came in," he says, placing his own cup of coffee on the table while leaning back in his chair, getting comfortable like we're here to meet for a coffee date.

"Where's my stuff?" I check the floor at his feet for the box or a bag, but there is nothing in sight.

"I left it in my trunk."

"You left it in your trunk," I repeat, sounding as annoyed as I feel. "Why didn't you bring it in here to me?"

"The box is falling apart. I didn't think you'd appreciate me leaving a trail of your photos on the sidewalk," he replies, taking a sip of coffee. "I'll get it for you when we leave here."

I open my mouth to tell him that the box wouldn't be falling apart if he had put it in a new box when he said he would mail it to me, but a shadow falls over the table and I glance up, blinking to make sure I'm not seeing things.

"Jamie?" I stand automatically to give my brother a hug, asking quietly, "What are you doing here?"

"I'll explain later." He kisses my forehead then glowers at Troy while moving a chair from another table, placing it with the back to the table between Troy and me before straddling it.

"How have you been, Jamie?" Troy asks with a hint of nervousness in his tone as he eyes my brother, who I have to admit looks intimidating. Not just because he's much larger than Troy. His leather jacket, shredded jeans, and heavy-looking black boots would make any normal person cower if faced with him.

"Been good, Troy. How have you been?"

"All right." He looks between Jamie and me. "I didn't think you'd be here."

"Funny, I didn't think you'd be here either." Jamie glances at me with a look that says I'm in trouble. "Last I heard, you were going to mail my sister her shit."

"I was going to," he agrees then clears his throat. "I just know how important the box is to her and wanted to make sure she got it."

"It's really nice of you to look after her like that, especially since you didn't seem to give a fuck how she would feel when you slept with someone else after your ring was on her finger."

"Jamie," I hiss.

He turns to glare at me. "Where's your box?"

"Jamie," I repeat, softer this time, knowing his temper and how quickly this could escalate.

He turns to look at my ex once more. "Where is her box, Troy?"

"It's in my car."

"Why don't you do me a favor and go get it," he suggests, and Troy stands without another word and heads across the room to the door.

After I see him exit, I look at my brother, finding him watching me. "Was that necessary?"

"You said you would tell me if he asked to meet up with you, Dakota. What the fuck?"

"Who told you I would be here?" I ask, and his eyes narrow.

"That's a whole other conversation we need to have. Why the fuck haven't you told me about the guy you're seeing?"

"Oh my God, I'm seriously going to kill him." I squeeze my eyes closed and rub my forehead. "I can't believe he called my brother, especially after our conversation last night. What the hell is wrong with him?"

"He's obviously worried about you," Jamie says, and my eyes open just enough to glare at him.

"Do not even think about taking his side on this, Jamie. You don't know him. You don't know the things he's done."

"Unlike you, *Dakota*, he talked to me, so yeah I do know."

"He told you he stole my digital information?"

"If that's your e-mail and shit, then yeah, he told me," he replies, not seeming concerned at all by the fact that Braxton has basically come into my life and stomped all over it. Then again, he doesn't know anything but what Braxton has told him. "I like him," he mutters, and I blink in disbelief.

"You like him?"

"Yeah. I like him."

"*You don't know him!*" I screech then take a few deep breaths, hoping to calm myself down before I cause a scene. I thought I might have finally gotten through to Braxton. I thought maybe, just maybe, me hanging up on him and not calling him back or returning his texts or e-mails this morning might have worked to make him realize he can't just take over anytime he wants to get his way. I guess I was wrong, and I also now know he has no limits. He will do whatever is necessary to get his way, including getting my brother on his side. My brother who has never liked any man I've ever dated.

"We'll talk after you get your shit," Jamie says, placing his hands over mine on the table, and I focus on him then jump slightly when my box is dropped before me, causing the table to shake.

I look from the box to Troy and can tell he wants to say something, but because of Jamie, he's unsure how to proceed. He runs a hand through his hair with his eyes locked on mine, and the look he gives me is filled with regret and sadness—two emotions that shouldn't make me feel sorry for him but still do.

"Thank you," I say softly.

"I'm sorry," he murmurs just as softly, and those old feelings I used to have for him come to the surface. I don't want him; I don't even like him anymore, but a part of me still cares about him and is disappointed he wasn't who I thought he was.

"I know. Me too," I agree with my throat tight, and he nods once before he turns around and leaves. I watch him go then duck my head, unwilling to allow the tears I feel burning the back of my throat to fill my eyes. I never got closure when it came to him. I never had a chance to ask him why he did what he did. One day, we were together, and I thought I was happy. Then the next, things between us were over and our lives were forever changed. I don't know if things would have lasted between us if he hadn't cheated, and I think that's one of the hardest things for me to come to terms with. It's always easy to hate someone when they have wronged you, but that doesn't mean you don't still care about them, even if you shouldn't.

"Dakota." Jamie touches my arm, and I yell at myself to pull it together before I lift my head to look at him. "Shit. Fuck, I'm sorry, sis," he whispers, and my shoulders shake as the pain in my chest expands.

I don't remember the last time I cried, but with everything that has been going on, I can't hold back the tears no matter how hard I try.

"I'm okay." I try to breathe, to attempt to get myself together, but the stupid tears continue to fall.

"Come on. Let's get you back home." Jamie stands, taking my box that is falling apart at the seams, and puts it under his arm before taking my hand and pulling me up. I stand with him then burrow into his side when he wraps his arm around me.

We walk down the block to my building with tears still falling from my eyes. Once we get inside, he leads us to the elevator, and then I let us into my apartment and head right for the couch, while Jamie goes to the kitchen. I listen to him fill my tea kettle, and then a few minutes later, he comes over to me with a cup of my favorite tea, setting it on the coffee table before sitting and placing my feet on his lap.

"I really fucking hate you're upset over that piece of shit," he mutters, slipping the blanket from the back of the couch to rest it over me.

"I'm not upset about him. Or it's not all about him," I say while leaning forward to grab the box of Kleenex from the table, tugging a couple out before lying back down and dabbing my eyes that have finally stopped leaking.

"Is it about Braxton?"

"Some." I swallow, not even sure myself. "I think it's everything—not getting closure with Troy, moving in to my own place, my job, my relationship with Braxton, and how there are times I want nothing more than to dive into things with him head-first, and others when he does stuff that makes me question if I should."

"Why didn't you tell me about him?" he asks, and the disappointment in his voice causes a fresh wave of tears to fill my eyes.

That's a good question. "I don't know," I admit while sitting up and grabbing my tea, needing the warmth and a moment to try to figure out my own thoughts. I've always talked to Jamie about everything going on in my life, but maybe a part of me didn't want to tell him the things I've had issues with when it comes to Braxton and didn't want Jamie to hate him before I've had a chance to figure out if I could possibly be falling for him. "I think I've been trying to figure out how I feel about him and didn't want to talk to you about him until I did."

"You like him."

I know it's not a question.

I lick my lips and nod once. "I do—most of the time anyway. When we're together without the outside world interfering, he makes me happy, he makes me laugh, and he makes me feel like I'm important, good enough." I pull in a deep breath. "But there are times when he makes me question my own sanity, times he does things I hate and get frustrated, because it's like he doesn't believe he's doing anything wrong."

His eyes narrow. "Things like what?"

I roll my eyes. "Like calling to tell you I was meeting up with Troy so you could show up." I shake my head. "Who does something like that?"

"He was worried about you, Dakota," he says, seeming to relax, like me thinking Braxton contacting him for the reasons he did is absolutely normal.

"Maybe that's why I didn't talk to you about

Braxton. You would do the insane things he has done if given a reason or the opportunity."

"If you mean protecting someone I care about, then hell yeah, I would."

I groan and lean back against the couch. "I'm surrounded by crazy people."

He grabs my foot and my attention. "If you tell me I shouldn't like him, I won't, Dakota. But I have to tell you he didn't sugarcoat shit for me. He told me about everything, even about lying to you the night you two met, something you didn't even tell me about."

My mouth drops open. "He told you about that?"

"He did." He smirks. "I mean, if you think about it, that shit is kind of funny."

I grab the pillow from behind me and toss it at his head. "It's not funny. Do you know how stupid I felt when I found out I spent the night with a man I didn't know then later on that he's actually the CEO of IMG, the company I just started working for?"

"I don't want to know about you two spending the night together," he mutters, looking disgusted.

"An amazing night together." I fight back my smile as his face pales. "Seriously, he's—"

"Shut up, Dakota." He throws my pillow back at me, making me laugh. "I never, ever want to hear about what you are doing with anyone behind closed doors."

"Oh, but it was okay for me to have to listen to you go at it all night with the random women you brought home?"

"It's not the same thing."

"Umm, yeah, Jamie, it is. Only it's worse having to hear the sounds your brother makes when he's—"

He covers my mouth before I can finish and glares at me. "Okay, fuck, I'm sorry. Just please stop."

"I'll stop," I mumble against his hand, and he lets me go before moving back in his seat, still glaring at me.

Giggling, I take a sip of my tea then rest it on my knee. Silence settles between us, and I jump when my cell in my bag starts to ring. I grab my purse off the floor where I dropped it and dig out my phone. When I see Braxton is calling, I don't hesitate to put it to my ear.

"If you think calling my brother won you any brownie points, you are seriously confused. I thought I was mad at you before. But now, I'm—" I try to come up with something worse than mad, but I'm so mad nothing comes to mind. "—I'm whatever comes after being mad. Maybe furious." I end the call before he can even respond and shut off my phone then look at my brother, who is watching me with an understanding look in his eyes. "What?"

"You know, when you were with Troy, no matter what he did, no matter how mad you were at him, you never once told him how you felt."

"I told him," I defend myself.

He shakes his head. "You didn't, Dakota, and I know there were times when you wanted to."

It's then I realize he's right. I never told Troy if he

made me mad, if he made me feel uncomfortable or like I couldn't be myself when I was around him or his family. When I was with him, I felt like I was the lucky one, like I was lucky he wanted me. I never once thought he was lucky to have me.

"I'm not saying what Braxton has done is right or that it's even okay, but I like that you don't have an issue telling him how upset you are, even with how much money he has, how much power he has. I think that says a lot. I think it shows just how much you trust him."

"Trust him?" I frown, thinking trust is a funny word to use when it comes to Braxton.

"I don't think that unless you trust someone you can ever truly express how upset you are with them and their actions. Showing any kind of emotion lets people know how much power they have over you, and being angry is one of the biggest emotions we will ever experience besides love. You can't show anger without trust, just like you can't feel love without trust."

"Are you saying I'm in love with Braxton?" The thought alone makes me want to run for the hills, but if I'm honest with myself, every time I'm around him, I feel more and more for him and am falling deeper and deeper into the connection we have with each other.

"All I'm saying is it's nice to see that you can be yourself with a man you obviously care about."

"When did you Mr. Anti-Relationship, Mr. Anti-Love become the spokesperson for what it takes to build a successful relationship?"

"I know jack shit about relationships. All I know is that you have to trust the person you are with; otherwise, you are both just wasting your time."

"You know, whenever you do decide to settle down, that girl is going to be lucky."

"I'm not so sure about that," he says, and I look into his eyes, seeing his own self-doubt, and set down my cup. I move toward him and rest my head on his chest then wrap my arm around his waist. "I'm lucky to have you, your support, and love, and I know that whoever you end up with will feel the same. You are an amazing man, Jamie. I'm lucky to have you in my life."

He wraps his arm around my shoulders then kisses the top of my head. "It's going to be okay. No matter what happens, we've got each other."

We've got each other. I know that, but I want more. I want a husband and a family, and part of me hopes Braxton is going to be a part of my story. I just really need him to prove he's capable of not acting on instinct and being the man I need him to be. We have enough drama between us without him adding more. I can admit I care about him, but I don't like that he's constantly doing things that make me feel like he has the upper hand.

"I think you should cut him some slack," he says, and I look up at him as he dips his head down toward me. "I'm not saying you should let him off the hook for the shit he's done, but part of me knows he's trying to find a way to make things work between you two. He cares about you."

"Don't you think it's a little insane how he's acted?"

"I don't know. I've never really cared about a woman besides you, so I can't say what I would do to make sure the person I cared about was safe."

"I don't need him to take care of me, Jamie, and I'm not doing anything that would put me in danger," I say, and his arm around me seems to tighten ever so slightly. "What. What is that?"

"I think you should give him a chance to explain himself," he replies before pressing his lips to the top of my head. "I don't want to go, but I need to meet up with Dan. We're supposed to finalize the schedule for the next few months." He lets me go and stands.

I want to ask him what his subtle reaction was about, if he knows something I don't, but I keep my mouth closed. He doesn't need to worry about me right now. In a way, his life is just starting, and I don't want to complicate that or make him feel like he needs to choose between me and his future.

"I'll be at your show Friday," I say quietly, getting up to walk him to the door.

"I'll be looking for you," he responds, and then he stops and turns to face me. "Call me—if anything happens or if you just need to talk."

My chest warms. "Thanks, big brother." I give him a hug then open the door.

With a lift of his chin, he's gone and I lock up. I look around my empty apartment and walk over to my bed, where I flop down face-first then roll to my back. I stare at the ceiling, thinking it's way too quiet, and worse, a little bit lonely.

"I should get a fish," I mutter to myself. I mean, I don't really think a fish is exactly good company, but at least it would be something. Maybe I'll become the fish lady, with a hundred fish tanks to take care of, since I don't think I can become a dog lady, not with how much time they require. And cats are out of the question, since I'm allergic, even though I wish I wasn't.

With a groan, I pull my pillow over my head. I must be more tired than I thought I was, because I wake up to an annoying buzzing sound in that exact position. I toss my pillow away and get up to stumble to the door half asleep, and I press the intercom when I get there. "Hello."

"Ms. Newton, I have a delivery for you. Are you available to accept it?"

I blink at the clock across the room and see it's six, around the time I usually get up to start getting ready for work.

"Ms. Newton, are you there?"

"Sorry, yes, you can bring it up." I release the button then walk into the kitchen and fill my teakettle, willing it to boil.

I yawn as there is a knock on the door, and when I open it, I don't know what I'm expecting, but it's not someone just handing me a card. I accept it with a quiet "thank you" then walk over to the couch and stare at the sealed envelope, flipping it over in my hands before finally ripping open the seal. I unfold the white piece of paper, and I swallow as I read the typed-out words.

I'm sorry,
Braxton

I want to believe him. I want to believe he really is sorry, but I'm not sure he even thinks what he did was wrong—not after everything he's done and continues to do. I ball up the paper in my hand and drop it to the floor at my feet. Then I get up and grab a cup of tea before going to get ready for work.

And when I get home that evening, I find a beautiful, brightly colored betta fish in a simple glass bowl on my kitchen counter along with a container of food. I tap the glass smiling then take off my watch and toss it into one of the drawers.

Chapter 11

$\mathcal{S}$TANDING IN MY bathroom with Samantha next to me, both of us primping to go out tonight for Jamie's show, I meet her gaze in the mirror and smile as she picks up her wineglass to take a sip. This week, we've spent a lot of time together, not just at work but we've had lunch together every day and went out for drinks a couple times. It's been nice having a friend, and I'm looking forward to having her with me tonight to keep me company.

"Can I ask you something?" she asks, and I laugh, because she already sounds a little tipsy. Then again, I might be a little tipsy myself.

"Sure."

"What's going on with you and Mr. Adams?"

At her question, I almost burn myself as I fumble

with my curling rod. Besides Samantha mentioning Braxton showing up at the bar, no one has questioned me. Not one person has even given me a funny look. It's like it never happened at all, and because of that, I kind of forgot it even did.

"Sorry, I shouldn't ask. I mean, it's not my business."

I wet my lips, unsure what to say. I want to be honest with her, because her question is something a friend would ask, but a part of me wants to keep the information to myself until I know where he and I are headed.

"I don't know," I say quietly. It's been days since I've spoken to him. Not that he hasn't attempted to contact me. I've just been working hard at ignoring his calls, texts, and e-mails, wanting time to try to figure out my feelings without his overwhelming presence interfering. I've figured out that I miss him and have even been grateful for his persistence during this time. It's made me feel like he hasn't forgotten me, like what we've shared is important to him, like *I'm* important to him.

"The night we met, I had no idea who he was." I set down my curler and pick up my glass of wine. "He lied to me. I was supposed to meet a blind date. I thought he was the guy and approached him, and instead of telling me he was the wrong man, he told me he was my date."

"Shut up," she whisper-hisses, and I shake my head with a giggle, like Jamie finding the humor in the situation now that I'm no longer angry about it.

"We went out and one thing led to another, and he stayed the night."

Her eyes are wide with horror. "Let me guess—you found out he lied the next morning."

I nod. "I found out he lied and lost my mind. Then later, I found out exactly who he is when I ran into him at the office. And since then, things between us have been complicated."

"I hate to tell you this, but it sounds like it's always been complicated."

"You're not wrong about that." I sigh, turning back to the mirror.

"Do you like him?"

"When he's not making me mad or doing things that make me crazy, I really like him. I've never met a man like him before. He's funny, sweet, and really kind, but he can also be pompous, demanding, and infuriating."

"Hot." She grins then continues, "And let's not forget gorgeous and sexy."

"We can't forget that." I laugh.

"Well, I think you guys look cute together, and I don't know him or what he's like, but I've dated a lot, and I can tell you that not once did a guy show up where I was because he wanted to spend time with me. Really, most of the men I've dated would be happy if I decided to go out with friends, so they could have some time alone or time to do whatever they wanted to do… including another girl."

I blink at her in surprise. She's gorgeous, with thick

dark hair, big blue eyes, full lips, and a body even the Kardashians with all their money would envy.

"Don't look at me like that." She shakes her head. "Dating nowadays is a joke. Everyone is looking for their next conquest, and I have yet to meet a man who is even a little interested in something serious."

"You're kidding."

"No. I mean a guy might say they are looking for a serious relationship on their dating profile, but at the end of the night, all they want is a quick fuck or a low-maintenance fuck buddy." She eyes me with disbelief. "Don't tell me you don't know that."

"I've only really been with two guys, my ex-fiancé and Braxton."

"Count yourself lucky. You've found two guys who want to commit while most of us can't even find one."

"I'm not that lucky, my ex fiancé cheated on me and I found out when I was in the middle of planning our wedding."

Her expression softens. "I'm sorry."

I shrug. "Me too, but I'm glad I found out before we actually got married or had kids."

"True," she agrees, the happy energy from earlier turning somber.

I shake my head. "Enough of that. Tonight is about having fun."

"Yeeesss, I need some fun." She holds up her glass, and I tap mine to hers then down the rest of my wine. We finish our hair and makeup then get dressed, me in a pair of ripped jeans and a sheer black top over my black bra with my leather jacket and pumps, and her in a skin-tight, off-the-shoulder black dress and thigh-high boots with a long black trench. We jump in a cab and head across town, and then because my brother and his band are performing, we walk in past the line of people who are waiting to get inside.

The moment we enter the bar, I latch onto Samantha's hand as the energy of the crowd, lights, and music seeps into my system. I'm sure to someone like my brother who lives off the high, it makes him feel alive, but for me, it's just overwhelming.

I lead Samantha to the bar, needing a drink, and it only takes a couple seconds for one of the bartenders to recognize me and come over. We both shout our orders, and moments later, we're heading toward the stage with our drinks. The opening act is performing, so I signal for Samantha to follow me backstage, and as soon as the bouncer lets us back, the sound is drowned out and I can hear myself think again.

We walk down the dim hallway toward the room where I know my brother and his band will be ignoring the catty looks from the groupies who are waiting, hoping to be seen. When we get to the door, I don't knock; I push right in and want to laugh. You would think the guys would be surrounded by women, hooking up, or getting high, but instead, they are all sitting in front of a large TV, playing some video game, and egging each other on while drinking from a bottle of Jack.

I stand at the back of the room, still holding

Samantha's hand, and wait for them to notice us. And then I clear my throat when it takes a while for anyone to pull their attention away from the game. Lozz, the lead guitarist, is the first to turn around, and when he does, he smiles his too-charming smile then slaps Jamie on his chest with the back of his hand.

My brother looks over his shoulder, and I wiggle my fingers. "I don't mean to interrupt."

"Took you long enough to get here." Jamie pushes off the couch and swaggers toward us then lifts me off my feet in a hug. Once he drops me back on solid ground, his eyes go to Samantha. "Who's this?"

I roll my eyes as he blatantly checks her out.

"Jamie, Samantha. Samantha, my brother Jamie." I look around the room at each of the men who seem to be fascinated with her. "Samantha is my friend, which means she's off-limits."

Jinx, the drummer, smiles and shows off a dimple. Lozz smirks like he knows I'll kick his ass but otherwise doesn't look like he gives a fuck. And Freddie, who plays bass, and has always been the more laid back one of the bunch just laughs.

"We work together, so be on your best behavior."

"I need a friend." Jinx winks at her, but before I have a chance to tell him not to be an asshole, Lozz knocks him upside his head. "What the fuck?" He glares at his bandmate while rubbing the back of his head.

"Show some respect. She's Dakota's friend," Lozz mumbles, coming over to give me a hug and to kiss

Samantha's hand and introduce himself, a move that makes me frown. I've seen Lozz basically drag women out of a room to go do God knows what with them. I've never once seen him kiss a woman's hand or act like he has even a bit of gentleman in him.

When Jinx and Freddie come over, I make introductions then look at my friend. At one glance, I can tell she's been struck by the bad-boy bug. I get it; these guys are all tall, broad, and good-looking with that tattooed look that tends to fascinate good girls who want to see if they can change their wicked ways.

"Are you okay?"

My brother's question drags my attention away from Samantha, and I focus on him.

"Yeah." I grab his upper arm in a reassuring gesture, but I'm not sure if I'm reassuring him or myself. He eyes me warily, and I wonder what that's about, wonder if he's talked to Braxton over the last few days. I don't ask. I don't want to know—or that's what I tell myself. "Are you ready for your show?"

"I'm always ready to hit the stage," he says, and I study him and can tell he's already pumped up. His pupils are slightly dilated, his body buzzing. He's excited, anxious to share himself with the crowd who has gathered to see him perform.

"There's a lot of people out there, and even more waiting to get in."

"Maggie will be happy about that. She's worried about losing us when we go on tour," he explains, and I realize then that I haven't spoken to Maggie in a while. Not that we were great friends, but we did text every now and then before I accidentally stood up her friend and got wrapped up in Braxton.

"Is she here tonight?"

"If she's not yet, she will be," he replies, looking at the door when someone knocks softly.

I turn at that time and see a cute girl with oversized glasses on poke her head into the room. "Maggie told me to let you guys know you're on in five," she says quietly, her cheeks turning pink.

"Thanks, Ally," Jamie replies, his voice gentle, and her face becomes an even deeper shade of pink before she nods and shuts the door.

"She's got it bad for you, dude," Jinx says, looking at Jamie, and I narrow my eyes on my brother.

"What?" he asks me.

"I just got a glimpse of her and know she is way too sweet for a guy like you. Don't even think about going there."

"It hasn't even crossed my mind." He holds up his hands when I raise a brow. "She's Maggie's niece and not my speed."

"You mean she's not easy." I roll my eyes, finishing my drink and setting the cup down.

"She's sweet, but like you pointed out, she's not for me."

"She might not be for him, but it's funny as shit to watch the two of them together, her stumbling all over herself, him trying not to scare her off." Jinx laughs.

"Shut the fuck up, man," Jamie grumbles then looks

at me. "Are you planning on hanging after the show?"

"Maybe, it depends on what Samantha wants to do." I glance over to where she and Lozz are sitting on the couch, talking.

"I'd guess she'd be cool with hanging out after."

I smack his arm. "She's not one of your groupies."

He grins. "It only takes seeing us perform once to become a groupie."

"Maybe you should get that printed on a T-shirt to sell at your concerts," I say, taking his bottle of Jack and putting it to my lips, coughing as the heat hits my throat.

He laughs, wrapping his arm around my shoulders. "I'm glad you came." He kisses the side of my head then lets me go and shouts, "Let's go!"

A minute later, the guys are heading toward the stage, with me and Samantha going back the way we came. As we exit backstage, the crowd roars at the first cords of their hit song, "Drink with Me." I look at Samantha and grin then lead her to the front of the stage.

"Holy shit, they are good!" she shouts at me three songs later, and I nod.

She's not wrong; they are good, and I really do think that once they hit the road, they are going to take the music industry by storm. I'm happy for my brother but a little sad for myself, because I know things between us are changing. We don't need each other as much as we once did. We're both becoming adults with our own lives and our own futures. Even if those futures seem to be up in the air right now.

Needing a minute away from the crowd, I lean into Samantha and shout in her ear, "I'm going to go to the bar. Do you want to come with me?"

"I think I'll stay," she says, her eyes locked on Lozz. "But will you bring me a vodka tonic?"

"Yeah," I shout back then push through the mass of people trying to get as close to the stage as possible. It takes me a few minutes to make it to the bar, and when I do, I yell, gaining the bartender's attention, then ask him for my order. When he disappears to fill it, I look to the stage and watch my brother do what he does best.

"Where the fuck have you been?" I turn at that question and find Maggie smiling at me.

"Work." I smile back, moving across the space to give her a hug.

"Well, I've missed seeing your face." She lets me go and smiles once more, letting me know she's not mad, that we're good. "You look amazing."

"Thanks." I tuck my hair behind my ear, swaying slightly.

"It's so funny you're here tonight, because Adam is here too," she tells me, and my heart sinks. "He should be here any second. He was just upstairs helping me with my computer."

"Maggie—" I start to tell her that I'm not interested in meeting her friend, but she looks over my shoulder and waves someone over.

"Adam, I want you to meet Dakota," she shouts

before she spins me around without giving me a choice, and I latch onto the person in front of me so I don't drunkenly fall on my face.

"It's nice to meet you too." He laughs, and I look up at him. Oh, God, Jamie was right! He looks like my ex—or at least his smile does.

"Sorry." I pull out of his hold and stick out my hand. "Dakota."

"Adam." He takes my hand, holding it tight while looking into my eyes. "It's nice to finally meet you."

"You too." I pull my hand away when someone whistles, startling me, and I wipe my palm down the front of my jeans. "Sorry about the whole date thing," I blurt, and he chuckles.

"It's okay. Maybe we can meet for coffee or a drink sometime."

"You're both here now and there is a bar a few feet away," Maggie chimes in, and I swear I could kill her.

"I…" I look over at the bar and see my drinks are ready. "I wish I could hang and talk, but I'm here with a friend of mine from work. I'm sorry."

"That's all right. I'll get your number from Maggie and we can set something up."

"Yeah, totally," I lie, just wanting to get away. "It was nice meeting you."

"You too, Dakota." He takes my hand and brings it to his lips, making me cringe.

"Okay, well, I'll see you." I discreetly wipe the back of my hand on my jeans then lean over and hug Maggie, who looks like she just did Cupid's job for him and is going to steal his title. "I'll talk to you soon."

"You will," she agrees, giving me a tight squeeze.

When she lets me go, I walk to the bar and pick up my drinks, leaving some cash, then head back to Samantha, wondering what the hell I will do if Adam calls. I mean, if I weren't drunk right now, I'd probably be freaking out, but the alcohol in my system is making me a little less worried about what might happen. With a sigh, I take a sip of my drink then shove back through the crowd.

I see Samantha searching for me over the sea of people, and as soon as I'm close, she yells, "I was just going to come search for you."

"Sorry, I ran into Maggie who owns this place and the guy I was supposed to go out with the night I met Braxton," I shout back.

She starts to choke on her drink, and I pound her on her back. "What? How did that go?"

"Maggie tried to get me to hang out with him tonight. I got out of it, but he said he would get my number from Maggie and call sometime."

"What are you going to do when he calls?" she asks, her eyes wide with concern.

"Tell him I'm seeing someone. I'm not going out with him, but I was on the spot and didn't want to hurt his ego."

"Girl, I need some of your man mojo." She laughs, taking a sip of her drink.

"I don't think you do." I look at the stage where

Lozz is playing the guitar.

"Oh no, no way. I would never date a guy like him," she says, shaking her head frantically.

"Okay, I'm going to try not to be offended by that statement. But I will tell you that Lozz is like family to me and he's a good man."

"Oh, God." She looks horrified. "I just mean that I don't think I could handle this." She motions around us. "The women, the attention. He seems nice, but I have trust issues when it comes to men, and this… all of this would be too much for me."

My face softens. "I can understand that." I wrap my arm around her shoulders. "Men really do fuck us up."

"Yeah, they do, but hopefully a good one will un-fuck us."

"Hopefully." I laugh.

"Dakota." My eyes widen when my name is called, not from the crowd but from the stage. I look at my brother, my face getting red as he motions for me to come up to him, and I shake my head. "Come on, sis."

I'm going to kill you, I mouth, walking to the stairs and climbing them slowly. When I reach him, he hands me the bottle of Jack.

"A little liquid encouragement," he says, and the crowd cheers and laughs. I put the bottle to my lips and fight the burn as I swallow. "Now, not many people know my sister can sing. I tried to get her to join my band, but instead, she went to college." He chuckles when the crowd boos. "Come on. Getting an education is important. Anyway, my sister and I didn't have it easy growing up, but we always had each other, and that's all we needed. This is a song we wrote together one night when we needed the power of music to get us through. So I think it's only right that she performs this one with me." He looks over at me. "Are you ready?"

"Are you giving me a choice?"

"No."

"Then, I guess I'm ready." I down another swig of Jack then lean into him when he wraps his arm around my shoulders and shoves the mic between us. The bass, guitar, and drums start, and I close my eyes, getting lost as I sing a sad song about two kids who lost everything but still had something to cling to. When the song comes to an end, I give him a hug then hustle off the stage and through the back doors while the crowd cheers. Needing a minute alone, I go to the bathroom and push into one of the stalls, closing the door behind me. I breathe deep through the pain in my chest, pain I somehow forgot about, pain that is almost unbearable even now.

"Dakota," a deep, familiar voice calls, making my heart pound.

It can't be Braxton. He's not supposed to be home until Sunday.

I wipe the wetness from my cheeks, expecting to find my mind is playing tricks on me when I open the door. I step out and lock eyes with the man I've been missing like crazy standing with his back to the door, his arms crossed over his chest and a look of pain in his eyes. "You're back."

"Come here," he orders, opening his arms, and I don't hesitate to go to him, wrap my arms around his waist, and rest the side of my head against his chest as a fresh wave of tears fill my eyes.

"I miss my parents," I whimper as his hand smooths over my hair and comes to rest on the back of my neck, his scent and warmth seeping into me. "Before the accident, before my dad died we we're happy, I grew up happy."

"I'm sorry, baby."

"Me too." I hold onto him and breathe through the tears soaking up his strength. "I missed this."

His hand tightens and he holds me closer. "I missed this too."

I nod and close my eyes, feeling like I could just fall asleep right here.

"I thought you weren't coming home until Sunday."

"My plans changed," he mutters, tugging my hair and forcing my head back to look at me. "I don't like not being able to talk to you."

I swallow. "Then I guess there are things both of us don't like."

"Hmm." He uses his free hand to capture my throat then slides it up to my jaw as his eyes search mine. "You make me insane, Dakota."

"Ditto, Braxton," I pant as he lowers his mouth to mine. My eyes slide closed at the first touch of his lips, and I open for him, greedy for his taste. He licks into my mouth, and I latch onto him a little tighter, the buzz of alcohol and his attention making me feel lighttheaded.

"Dakota?" Samantha knocks on the bathroom door, and Braxton pulls away, groaning.

"That's Samantha," I tell him, then call out, "Just a second."

"Come away with me tonight," Braxton says, gaining my attention.

"I'm here with Samantha."

"Spend time with her then come away with me," he urges, and I study him and the look of longing in his eyes and nod. When he opens the door and Samantha sees him, her eyes widen.

"Braxton is here," I point out the obvious.

"Ms. Shelton," he says, and I elbow him then shake my head.

"We're not at work. You don't have to be so formal."

He smiles at me then looks at her. "Sorry, Samantha."

"It's okay." She laughs then looks between the two of us. "If you two want to take off you guys don't have to stick around for me. I can catch a cab home."

"Sounds good," Braxton murmurs.

"I'm not ditching you." I glare at the man behind me and she laughs.

"Really, it's okay. I think I've had enough fun for one night, probably more fun than I've had in forever."

"It was fun. We will have to do it again."

"Yes we will," she agrees and then looks down the hall, as there is a commotion. I look that way and see my brother and the guys coming our way. Nervousness settles in my stomach, and I hold my breath as they approach.

"Let me guess—you're Braxton," Jamie says, looking at the man who has moved to my side, and then the two of them shake hands and do that guy pat on the back thing. "Did you catch any of the show?"

"A few songs," Braxton replies, taking my hand and I know then he heard me sing with Jamie.

"Cool." Jamie looks at me and his face softens. "Are you okay?"

"Yeah," I respond, and Braxton squeezes my fingers in silent support.

"Are you heading out? Or are you going to stick around for a drink?"

I really don't think I need to have another drink. Honestly, everything is a bit hazy right now, but something is telling me that Jamie needs to see me with Braxton.

"Want to stay for a little longer?" I ask, taking Samantha's attention away from Lozz.

"Sure." She shrugs.

"We can stay for a few," I agree, looking at my brother.

"Come on then." He motions for us to follow, and I look up at Braxton as everyone heads down the hall.

"Are you okay with this?"

"You spending time with your brother and friends?" he prompts, and I nod. "Yeah, I'm okay with that." I lean up on my tiptoes and touch my mouth to his. When I start to pull back, he stops me. "But tonight, we're going to have a long talk about us, Dakota."

I lick my lips, not sure if I'm excited about having another talk with him, because part of me is scared everything between us will change, that we will never be able to agree on how things should be.

"I'm really looking forward to that," I say sarcastically, and he smiles then lets me go and smacks my ass. "Hey, that stung!"

"Oh, beautiful girl, you have no idea the things I'm going to do to you when I get you alone." He shakes his head and my body pulses. "Let's go spend time with your brother so I can reassure him that you're safe with me."

"I knew that's why he wanted us to stay," I grumble, and he laughs then takes my hand. We head into the room that we were in earlier, and within thirty minutes, my nervousness about Jamie and Braxton getting along is gone. The two of them talk and joke like they're old friends, and Braxton wins over his bandmates like he's one of them, all but Freddie who is sitting alone drinking. Normally I would go out of my way to talk to him but tonight his mood seems dark so instead I sit with Samantha sipping a fresh drink. I smile when I hear my brother laugh at something Braxton said and turn to look at him.

"I shouldn't be surprised that a man who wears a suit like a second skin can win over a bunch of rowdy rockers, but then again, it just goes to show how down to earth and laid back he is," Samantha says, and I look at her. "It's also probably why he's as successful as he is. He can blend in in any environment and make people feel he's just like them."

"He is just like them," I tell her quietly. "He's just a guy."

"And that right there is why he's falling in love with you," she whispers, and my heart seems to double-beat. "You don't see him as a billionaire. To you, he's just a guy you like."

"He's not falling in love with me," I deny, and she smiles.

"Yeah, and I bet you'd tell me you're not falling in love with him either."

I don't answer her. I look across the room, and when I do, his eyes come to me and his expression softens into a look I know I wouldn't mind seeing from him every day for the rest of my life.

Chapter 12

DAKOTA

$\mathcal{I}$ COME OUT of the haze of sleep hearing birds chirping, each tweet making my head pound a little harder. I cover my eyes with the crook of my elbow, despising the blinding light burning my eyelids, then breathe in through my nose, smelling wet pine and earth as a cool breeze skims my skin. If I didn't feel the soft bed under me, I'd wonder if I fell asleep outside in one of the parks near my building.

I try to remember last night, but it's choppy, only bits and pieces coming together—laughing, drinking, Braxton, and my friends. I work up the courage to uncover my face and force open my eyes, seeing wooden beams above me, and then turn my head, finding the bed behind me empty. I glance around the sparsely decorated room, a room I've never been in before.

Another piece of my missing night falls into place as I remember Braxton loading me into his car with my brother's help, the two of them arguing about me drinking too much and whose fault it was—something I thought was hilarious at the time.

I slowly sit up then look down at myself and the oversized white T-shirt I'm wearing, bringing it to my nose and smelling Braxton. After a minute, I stand and walk to the open window. I'm on the second floor, judging by the view of the forest outside, and my guess is this is the cabin Braxton mentioned to me. I go to the first door I see and am grateful when I find it's a bathroom.

I step in and cringe when I see myself in the mirror. My makeup is smeared and my hair is a mess. I quickly start up the shower then use the toothpaste and brush in the holder next to the sink to get rid of the alcohol I can still taste on my breath. I use the few items in the shower to wash up then shut off the water and get out, looking for a towel. Not finding one, I give up and put the shirt back on, leaving my panties off. Still dripping wet but feeling a little better, I step out of the room and stop.

Braxton's idea of a small cabin and mine are vastly different. The space below me is huge with a large kitchen and living room with a comfortable-looking couch, a stone fireplace, and a pool table. The living space is nice, but what has my attention are the windows that show the world outside from the floor to the ceiling that must be thirty feet high.

I take a step, wrap my hands around the rough-cut log banister, and watch Braxton in the kitchen with his back to me, wearing nothing but a pair of sweats with his phone to his ear as he turns eggs over in a pan. Another memory falls into place, making me want to turn around and go back into the room to hide. Last night, he told me he wanted to talk, and at the time, I wasn't looking forward to that. But hung-over me is looking forward to that even less.

"Are you going to come down here and kiss me or are you going to stand up there staring out into space all day?" His words make me smile, and I focus on where he's now standing with his hands on the counter, leaning into it and looking up at me with his muscular torso, making my mouth water.

"I wasn't staring out into space. I was taking in the view," I defend myself as I head across the landing and down the stairs to the first floor. He meets me when I reach the last step and pulls me into his arms, kissing me softly before leaning back to frown down at me.

"Why is your shirt wet?"

"I showered," I state the obvious, touching my still sopping wet hair. "There were no towels in the bathroom."

He drops his eyes to my chest, and I watch them grow dark. "I ran them through the wash the last time I was here. They're in the dryer," he says, brushing the back of his fingers across the front of my shirt over my nipple. I bite my lip to keep from moaning, and his eyes meet mine as I shiver. "As much as I enjoy you wet, let me get you something to put on." He kisses me swiftly then moves around me to go up the stairs. "I made breakfast, and there's coffee in the pot. Help yourself, and I'll be back in a second."

I cross my arms over my chest and walk toward the kitchen but make a beeline for the living room when I see the coffee table that is sitting in front of the couch. The wood looks similar to his table in the city, but in the open grooves and naturally pitted pieces, there is emerald-colored glass overlaid with lacquer, making the surface of the table look like glass. It's beautiful, and if he made something like this for his mom, I can see why she would hang it on her wall.

I turn when I hear him come down the stairs and notice he has a towel in hand along with another shirt, this one gray. "This is beautiful." I motion to the table, and he smiles softly. "If you ever want to quit your job, you could go into woodworking."

"I'll keep that in mind." He comes toward me then before I have time to prepare, he drops the towel to the couch and his hands are on my hips. "Arms up," he orders, and I lift my hands up over my head as he drags the wet shirt up my body then drops it to the couch. Without a bit of shyness, I keep my hands up as he places the dry one over my head.

"Thanks," I whisper, dropping my hands to my sides to rest over his on my hips.

"I wouldn't want you to get sick because of me."

"I don't think that's a thing," I whisper, my heart

beating hard as I try to understand how this guy can be so completely complicated. Hard and soft, sweet and hot, demanding and giving, everything I appreciate and despise in one gorgeous package.

"I think my mom would beg to differ." He lets his hands fall from my waist then picks up the towel. "Hold up your hair." I do, and he wraps the towel around my shoulders. Once it's in place, I let my hair fall and then rest my hands against his warm chest. "Are you hungry or just hung-over?"

"A little of both."

"Let's put something in your stomach then get you some Tylenol." He leans in to kiss my forehead then takes my hand from his chest and walks me to one of the barstools that form a half circle around the kitchen. I take a seat and then watch him as he makes me a plate piled high with eggs and pancakes he pulls out of the oven. He places my plate before me along with a set of silverware then sets out syrup and butter. "Coffee or tea?"

"Tea if you have it." I stand to wrap the towel around my hair as he turns on an electric kettle on the counter before getting a packet of my favorite tea and a cup. "I feel like you're always taking care of me."

"You're saying that like it's a bad thing."

Am I? Maybe. "I'm just not used to anyone but Jamie looking out for me."

"It's okay to trust someone besides your brother," he says, filling the cup with steaming water and placing the teabag inside. "You can trust me."

"I want to." I hold his gaze so he knows I really do want that, maybe even more than he does.

He studies me, his eyes searching mine, then clears his throat. "We need to talk."

My stomach drops, but I straighten in my chair, willing myself to stay strong and to be honest. "Okay."

"When it comes to you, I don't know what I'm doing." The statement is one I've heard from him before, and I wonder where he's going with this. "For a man like me, who's in control of every aspect of his life, you have sent my life into a tailspin. I don't know up from down. I can't sleep. I can't eat. I'm always worried about you, thinking about you, hoping you're sleeping and eating, that you're safe and happy."

I want to smile, because I can see he's annoyed with his own feelings and really doesn't know how to deal with them. "So… you're mad at me?"

His brows drag together and his lips turn down at that question. "Mad at you? No. I'm pissed at myself, because I keep doing things that I know will piss you off, but I can't help it, because at the end of the day, I want to reassure myself that you're okay."

"And what is it you think will happen to me if you don't have control when it comes to me?"

"I don't know." He rests his hands on the counter and his knuckles turn white, like he doesn't like the things his mind comes up with.

"Do you understand that all it does when you overstep is push me away and make me want to rebel?"

"I'm learning that," he grumbles, not sounding

happy about that either.

I get up off my stool and walk around the kitchen to him, and he turns toward me once I'm close. I place my hands on his chest and lean into him. "I don't want to be controlled, Braxton. That might be something I'm okay with in the bedroom, but when it comes to life, I don't want someone telling me what to do. I want a partner. I want a man who will listen to what I want and need, someone to share things with."

"You can share things with me." He settles his hands on my waist and drags me against him.

"Can I?" I shake my head, trying not to become frustrated, because so far he's proven I can't. "You sent my brother to come to the coffee shop where I was meeting Troy, and that was something I didn't even tell you about." I feel his hands wrap tight into my shirt at my sides and watch his face get hard.

"He cheated on you. You don't need to be alone with him."

"I was in a public place, and I was meeting him to get my stuff—not for a date or to talk about us getting back together. And again, I never told you I was meeting him. You found out, because you used information I didn't give you." His jaw tics, and I know I've proven my point. Thank God, maybe we can actually get somewhere this time.

"Why didn't you tell me about meeting up with him?"

Okay, maybe not. "Because I knew that if I did, there would be drama, and I was over dealing with drama."

"You didn't tell Jamie either," he says like he's just made his point, when he most definitely has not.

"Yeah, because I know my brother, and like you, he would make the situation more complicated and uncomfortable than it needed to be, which he did when he showed up."

"I'm not going to apologize for that," he states, lifting me up onto the counter and forcing his way between my knees. "Jamie told me he didn't even have your stuff, that he left it in his car, which I'm sure was a move he made in order to get more time with you."

"Do you think I don't know that?" I roll my eyes and push on his chest. "I'm not stupid or helpless, Braxton. I know how to take care of myself."

"I never said you were stupid or helpless, but if I can do something to reassure myself that you're okay, I'm going to do it, and I won't apologize afterward."

"You did apologize," I remind him. "You sent me a note that said you were sorry.

"Sorry about you being upset. Sorry I'm so fucking obsessed with you that I will go to whatever lengths to get even the smallest piece of information about you. Sorry that I want you to myself and wish I could lock you away until you became as obsessed with me as I am with you."

"You do know that just being you—not the crazy you, but the sweet, funny, and adorably frustrating you—is doing that, right? You don't have to be so extreme."

He lowers his head and kisses my neck. "I can try."

"Try?" I ask, and he pulls back to meet my gaze.

He rests his forehead against mine. "I think I told you before, baby. I don't want to lie to you anymore, and I know telling you what you want to hear would be a lie. All I can do is promise I'll try to loosen up a bit."

I close my eyes and slide my hands up his chest, around the back of his neck, and through his hair, cupping the back of his head.

"Okay." I lean up, and he closes the distance, touching his lips to mine. "I want this to work, Braxton. I want this crazy, intense thing between us to work just as much as you do."

"Good." He slides his hands around my hips and down to cup my ass, and then he lifts me off the counter.

"Where are we going?"

"I need to be inside you." He kisses up my throat to my neck as I wrap my legs around his hips.

I hold tight to him as he carries me across the room then moan as he covers my mouth with his and lays me on the couch. And as we devour each other, I try to make him understand with every touch, lick, kiss, and sound that he's already got me, that I'm already obsessed with him.

WITH A FIRE burning in the fireplace casting a glow around the room, I lay with my head on Braxton's bare chest, my fingers smoothing over his side, his traveling idly up and down my back. I close my eyes.

It's Saturday night, and tomorrow morning, we're supposed to go back to the city, something I wish we didn't have to do. It's been a good day, one in which the outside world hasn't had a chance to interfere, where we've just been able to be us.

"I really wish we didn't have to go back tomorrow," I whisper into the quiet.

"I know." His lips rest against the top of my head. "If my parents weren't coming into town, we could spend another night and leave Monday morning, but we can come back next weekend if you want."

I tilt my head back to look at him. "Maybe you can show me more than the bedroom, the couch, and kitchen next time we're here." I grin. "I didn't even get to see your shop."

"Are you complaining about how you spent your day?" He rolls me to my back and settles between my legs.

"No." I smile, sliding my fingers through his hair, and lift up to touch my mouth to his. Just when the kiss starts to get hot, his phone rings, making me sigh.

"Sorry."

"It's not easy being the boss," I grumble, thinking next time we're here I'll lock his phone in his glove box where he can't hear it.

He smirks and touches his mouth to mine. "Be right back."

I get up on my elbow and watch him walk to the kitchen then decide now is as good of a time as any to go use the restroom. I stand, pick up my T-shirt, and put it on before padding to the bathroom. After I finish, I step out and frown when I don't see him in the kitchen on his phone, where he's taken most of his calls today.

I start to go in search of him but stop when I see him standing outside on the deck, still on his phone. Knowing if he went outside that he wanted privacy, I go to the kitchen to get some water then grab my phone out of my bag. I sit at the island and respond to the texts I have from Jamie and Samantha then play one of my word games, wishing I had my computer so I could check on my schedule for the week.

When the sliding glass door opens a few minutes later, I turn to watch him come back inside and can tell by the look on his face that he isn't happy. "What's wrong?"

He doesn't answer at first; instead, he closes the distance between us and takes my hand, resting it on his chest. "I'm sorry, baby, but that was the building manager. There was a problem, and they need me to come in to deal with it."

"What kind of problem?" I ask, not liking the amount of tension I can see in his frame.

"Nothing you need to worry about." He drops a quick kiss to my forehead then orders, "Let's get dressed and lock up here."

"Okay," I agree, trying not to be disappointed that he doesn't want to talk to me about what's going on.

It doesn't take us long to get packed up and into his Benz, and as he drives us into the city, the silence is heavy. I don't know what he's thinking about, but I'm wondering why it feels like he's keeping something from me.

When we reach our building, he drives into the underground parking lot, and then we get out and go to the private elevator. He waves his watch over the sensor and his floor lights up. Annoyed and just wanting to be in my space, I press the button for my floor.

"You're staying with me tonight," he informs me, and I cross my arms over my chest.

"You're going to be gone, so I want to sleep in my bed."

"I won't be gone all night. I want you in my bed when I get home," he says, glancing at his watch.

"No," I refuse, and he growls, the sound putting me on edge.

"Dakota."

"Braxton, if you want, you can come to my place when you're done doing whatever it is you're doing."

"You're staying at my place."

"I'm not." I shake my head. "I want to take a shower in *my* shower with *my* stuff and put on *my* clothes, and then go to bed in *my* bed," I tell him, and just then the elevator doors open for my floor. He steps in front of me to block my way, but I duck under his arm and walk quickly down the hall. When I turn the corner, my step falters when I see a police officer standing outside my apartment door.

"What's going on?" I ask, walking toward the cop.

"Dakota." Braxton grasps my upper arm and spins me around to face him.

I study him, trying to understand why he looks so freaked. "What happened?"

"The apartment below you called the building manager tonight to tell them there was water leaking into their apartment. They went into your place to check where the water was coming from and found your place had been vandalized."

"What?" My heart drops into my stomach, and I look over my shoulder at the officer who's watching us.

"Please just let me deal with this," Braxton pleads, and I focus back on him.

"It's my apartment and my stuff. I want to see." I pull from his grasp and head down the hall with him right behind me. When I reach the officer, he looks at the man at my back for approval, which pisses me off, but then he steps out of the way.

I walk into my place and can't even believe what I'm seeing. The entire space is destroyed, the floor covered with water, the couch cushions cut open, fuzz and foam littering the floor, my clothes ripped and strewn across the room and filling the sink, the photos and things from the box I got from Troy tossed across the wet ground like garbage. I barely even register the other people in the room and the quiet sound of conversation. My mind is consumed with the destruction surrounding me.

I take a step up to my bed and feel sick when I see

my underwear and bras placed on the bed in matching sets, the only items that seem to be laid out with care.

"Baby." Braxton takes my hand, and I look up into his worried eyes.

"Who did this?"

His expression grows dark, and his hold on my hand gets tight. "I don't know, but I'm going to find out."

My eyes scan my place, knowing that if anyone has the ability to find out who did this, he does.

"Mr. Adams." A man I don't recognize approaches us. "The police have a few questions," he says, looking at Braxton, and then his gaze comes to me. "I'm sorry, Ms. Newton."

"Thank you."

"Tell them I'll be a few minutes, Jimmy. I want to take Dakota upstairs and get her settled in my place," Braxton tells him, and he nods before turning and walking away.

I turn to face Braxton, and his eyes come to me. "I'm not leaving."

"Dakota."

"Braxton." I use his same frustrated tone. "I'm not leaving. This is my home. I want to talk to the cops."

"You need to tell her."

At that comment, my spine stiffens. I turn and watch Hanna come toward us.

"Tell me what?" I glance between her and Braxton, trying to understand the silent conversation they're so obviously having. "Tell me what?" I repeat when neither of them speaks.

Braxton lets out an annoyed breath then looks down at me. "The first time you were on air, the call center got a call from a man who made some unusual comments, and per protocol, they made a note and passed it along. It's not unusual for that kind of thing to happen from time to time in this industry, but each time you were on air, we were notified that the man would call back, and he seemed to be escalating." He turns me to face him and takes my other hand. "On Thursday, a package addressed to you was intercepted."

"And?" I whisper, unsure if I want to know.

"The items inside were disturbing, and the package was passed along to the police."

"You think whoever sent that package did this?" I ask.

He glances around my destroyed apartment. "I don't know, but with the calls and the package, it seems to fit."

"You never told me."

His eyes come to me, and I know the instant his warm gaze meets mine that he didn't tell me, because he didn't want me to worry. Like Jamie, he wants to protect me. The puzzle pieces begin to fall into place— all the times he's tried to convince me to move to the marketing department, his overbearing protectiveness. It's all been because he wanted me off air; he wanted to tuck me away in hopes that it would keep me safe.

God, this crazy, crazy man.

I hold his gaze and whisper, "Let's go talk to the cops."

Without a word, he leads me across the room to one of the officers, and then for the next hour, I try to make sense of what is happening.

But quickly, I realize I might never understand, yet it's time I trust the man who has stolen my heart.

Chapter 13

I SIT ON the floor in the living room in the dark and look out at the city below me, watching my breath fog up the glass as my forehead rests against it. I should be exhausted after the day I've had, but I can't sleep, which is why I carefully untangled myself from Braxton's hold and escaped to his living room to think. No matter what I do, I can't make sense of what happened to my apartment, and I can't even comprehend someone being so infatuated with me that they would go to such an extreme to get my attention.

The cops asked me tonight if I had anyone in my life or in my past who I would consider a suspect, and I honestly couldn't think of one person. Troy would be an obvious suspect, but I know he wouldn't risk tarnishing his family's name by being so devious, and there is no one else in my past who I can think of who would want to hurt me or given me a reason to believe they are even the slightest bit obsessed with me.

I close my eyes. Neither the police nor Braxton told me what was said on the phone calls or what was in the package they received, but by the looks that were passed around, I know whatever it was, it was bad. I also know Braxton well enough to understand he's not going to let me go about my life as usual, and I'm not sure I want to. For the first time in a long time, I feel vulnerable, the same kind of unease I felt as a kid when things in life were up in the air.

I open my eyes when I hear movement behind me then moments later, Braxton settles on the ground at my back and wraps his arms around me. Once I'm resting against his chest, encircled in the safety of his hold, I turn to my side to rest on my hip with my ear over his heart and listen to the steady beat.

"This is why I didn't want you to know what's been happening." His words cut through the silence, and I open my eyes.

"You don't think I would have eventually found out my place had been broken into and all my stuff was destroyed?"

"I was going to cross that bridge when I got to it."

"You're really unbelievable." I tip my head back, and he dips his head down to meet my gaze. "What was your plan? Were you going to just move me in with you and say you got rid of all my stuff?"

"Maybe." He sighs, and I want to laugh, because

he would do something so ridiculous in order to hide what happened, but all that would've done is create more issues between us.

"That would have been a lie," I point out.

"I know," he agrees.

"You said you don't want to lie to me anymore."

"I also don't want you so worried that you sneak out of bed in the middle of the night because you can't sleep."

"You can't stop me from worrying about this." I sigh, resting my head back against his chest.

"I know." He cups my jaw, smoothing his thumb back and forth over my cheek. "What took you from bed?"

"I just keep wondering what I did," I admit quietly as I stare at the silent street below us.

"You didn't do anything. Sometimes people are just mentally unable to distinguish the difference between real life and what they believe in their minds."

"I guess you're right."

"It will be okay." His lips linger on the top of my head as he continues to speak. "The police will do their job, and I have people looking into things as well. Until they find out who is behind the calls and what happened at your apartment, we will keep you off the air."

"I need to tell Jamie what happened."

"He knows about the calls."

He does? I mean that's probably what his strange looks were about and why he didn't seem to mind when I told him about Braxton's overprotectiveness. "I'm surprised he didn't demand he stay with me or something." He clears his throat, and I know there's more he's not saying. "What?"

"He also knows I've had someone watching you."

"You what?" I shout and attempt to push away from him, but when he doesn't let me go, I growl in frustration and give up. "Since when have you had someone watching me?"

"The morning after we met, I was informed about the phone calls, and when your name was mentioned, I decided to hire someone to watch over you while I was out of town. They have been following you since then."

"The big guy?" I ask, and he nods. "I knew it. So it was him who followed me in a car that morning?"

"No." He frowns. "Someone followed you in a car?"

"Yeah… or I think so." I shake my head. "I'm not sure. After I ran into you, I didn't see them again and thought I was imagining it."

"I think we need to tell the police about that incident. Do you remember what the car looked like?"

I try, but I can't recall. "I think dark, but I can't remember. It seems like forever ago."

"Has anything like that happened since then?"

I think about it, but "No."

"Before you moved here, did you ever receive any strange phone calls or letters, anything like that?" he asks—the same question the police asked me last night.

"No, I mean—" I pause, wondering if the photos of Troy cheating could be connected, but that was a long time ago. Surely something would have happened since then if they were.

"What?"

"The photos of Troy cheating on me came in a plain, unmarked envelope. I still don't know who sent them to me."

"Did Troy know who might have sent them? Maybe the woman he was cheating on you with?"

"I never asked. I've never even talked to him about what happened."

"Do you still have the pictures or the envelope?"

"No, I left them along with my engagement ring when I left."

"Troy's father is in politics. Someone might have been planning on using those pictures to blackmail him. I'll have my guys look into it. It might be connected, but it might not."

"You know Troy's dad is in politics?" I ask, and he raises a brow like *"Are you really asking that?"* "Right, never mind. Don't even bother answering that question. Of course you know."

His arms tighten around me. "I think you need to tell Jamie about what happened last night face-to-face. Maybe you can invite him over here and we can talk to him together, put him at ease, and make sure he knows you're safe."

"Your family is going to be here," I remind him of

something that has me nervous, especially since I'm not exactly in the best place mentally to meet them.

"What does that matter?"

"Because Jamie will probably lose his mind, and I'm not sure that is something you want your family to witness."

"You don't think my parents are going to be upset about this when they find out? My mother will probably demand I send you to stay with her, and my father will most likely ask if I want one of the guns he keeps locked away in his safe at home."

"Or your parents will think I'm bringing trouble to their son's doorstep and hate me because of it."

"No one is going to hate you." I see his lips twitch like he wants to laugh.

"You don't know that, and if they do, it's something you *for once* have no control over. You can't force them to like me."

"Let's just see what happens." He touches his lips to mine then stands and picks me up. "Right now, let's get some rest. We will have enough drama to deal with in the morning without making shit up tonight."

"I'm not tired," I tell him as he walks us into his room and lays me on the bed.

"Then you can just lie here with me," he bosses, climbing into bed with me and tucking his face against the crook of my neck. "You should know," he whispers as my body starts to relax, "my parents are going to love you, because they will see how happy you make me."

"I thought I just made you crazy."

"You do make me crazy." He kisses my neck. "But you make me happy too. You've given me something I didn't know I was missing until you came along. You've reminded me what's important, that it's the little things that matter most," he says quietly as my throat gets oddly tight. "I forgot that along the way, forgot how good it feels to laugh, to relax and just be myself." He laces his fingers through mine and brings our joined hands up to rest between my breasts. "I know I can't stop you from worrying, but just know that no matter what happens, you're mine and nothing is going to change that, because I refuse to give you up. And I will always keep you safe."

"And do I get a say about you keeping me?"

"If it's to disagree with me, no," he replies, and I hear the smile in his voice.

"Then I guess it's a good thing I like it exactly where I am."

"I guess so." He kisses my neck once more and silence settles over us, his breath growing soft and even.

When I know he's asleep, I roll over to face him and rest my hand on his cheek, whispering my truth into the dark. "I didn't forget, because I never knew this kind of happiness existed before you came into my life and turned it upside-down." I trace the edge of his jaw then tuck myself against his chest and close my eyes, knowing that even if I don't fall asleep, there is nowhere else I want to be but right here in his arms.

"I HATE YOUR phone," I groan, waking up to the annoying ringtone I know is attached to Braxton's cell. "I swear I'm going to shove that thing down the disposal and turn it on." I hear the man I'm still curled up against chuckle, and I open one eye to glare at him. "I'm not joking."

"Sorry, babe, it's work." He touches his lips to mine then rolls out of bed.

I pull his pillow over my head while shouting, "It's always work! Being the CEO is a stupid job, especially if you can't even take Sunday off to sleep in and relax."

I listen to him laugh then a moment later hear the door close as he leaves the room. I try to go back to sleep, wanting nothing more than to stay here the rest of the day hidden away, but thoughts of his parents coming, the call I have to make to Jamie, and going down to my place to try and salvage some of my stuff plagues me.

With a groan, I toss his pillow away and get out of bed. I go to his shower and turn it on. While the water warms up, I use his toothbrush and paste to brush my teeth, making a mental list of all the things I need to pick up at some point today. I know for sure I will not be wearing any of the undergarments I had in my apartment. I don't even want to imagine what was done to or with them. I also need some clothes, shower stuff, makeup, and I'm sure even more I won't remember until I need it.

After I get out of the shower, I wrap one towel around myself then another around my hair and open the door that leads to the closet. The room is big enough to be someone's bedroom and looks like a small men's department store. I start to open drawers to find something to wear and pause when I find a one drawer is nothing but ties that all look the same, just in different shades of gray, black, and navy-blue. With a shake of my head I close that drawer then open the rest until I find a pair of boxers, socks, and a T-shirt. I get dressed then go back to the bathroom, taking the towel from my head and hanging it up. Since I don't have a brush and all I can find is Braxton's comb, I run my fingers through my wet hair, trying to get most of the knots out, a task that feels hopeless with two days of not using conditioner.

"My parents are going to be up here in less than thirty minutes. They called when they were crossing the bridge into the city," Braxton says, patting my ass as he walks past me, and my eyes widen in horror as he continues to speak from the closet he disappears into. "I told my mom you're here. She's excited to meet you."

I look around the room for somewhere to hide then shake my head. I don't need to hide here. I have an apartment just a few stories down. I leave the bathroom and go in search of my phone and bag so I can get into my apartment, for the first time wishing I wouldn't have taken off my stupid watch, because I could use it to get into my place. Not finding my stuff in the bedroom, I go to the kitchen then the living room and the office I found the last time I was here.

"Can I ask what it is you're looking for?" Braxton asks casually, and I turn, finding him leaning against the counter in the kitchen, drinking a cup of coffee.

"I need my bag and my phone," I tell him, going back to search under the couch, since I didn't look there.

"Why do you need your purse?"

I rest my hands on my hips, breathing heavy. "I need to go home."

"You're not going home," he states, taking a sip of his coffee.

I stomp my foot. "Braxton, right now is not the time for you to tell me what I can or can't do. I need to go home. I haven't used conditioner in two days and I'm not meeting your parents for the first time while wearing your underwear."

"Conditioner?"

"Girls use it after they wash their hair. If they don't, their hair looks like mine did yesterday when it dried."

"What was wrong with your hair yesterday?" He frowns.

"Oh my God." I toss my hand into the air. "That is not the point! The point is I need to find my bag so I can go home, so where is it?"

"I don't know where your bag is." I narrow my eyes on his, trying to figure out if he's lying. "Did you leave it at the cabin or in my car last night?"

Did I? Shit. I don't know if I did or not. "Where are

your car keys? I'll go down and check your car." When he doesn't make a move to help me, I start to search for his keys, swearing I'm never, not ever, going to take off my watch ever again.

"If you were wearing your watch, you wouldn't need your phone or your purse," he informs me smugly, like he just read my mind, and I turn just enough to glare at him. He holds up his cup of coffee. "I'm just saying, baby. I came up with the applications in that watch to prevent situations just like this."

"I hate you," I mutter, ignoring his laughter as I go to the bedroom to search there.

After going through his drawers, dirty laundry, and checking under every surface in the bedroom, I stomp into the kitchen and plant my hands on my hips. "I'm going to ask you nicely to give me your keys, and if you don't, I swear I'm going to kill you and deal with the consequences later."

"Baby, I'd like you to meet my parents." He smiles, and I swear I feel the blood drain from my face and my stomach plummet. I close my eyes, hoping he's joking, but when I hear a woman laugh and a man chuckle, I know he's not. I slowly open my eyes back up and then pivot on my toes to face the island that surrounds the kitchen. Standing behind the bar is a man and woman, both attractive, both with features they have passed down to their son. "Mom, Dad—" Braxton comes to me, taking my hand. "I'd like you to finally meet Dakota. Dakota, my parents, Bret and Alisha Adams."

"I promise I didn't mean I would really kill your son," I blurt, feeling their eyes bore into me. "I just… I just…."

"Do you know how many times I threatened Braxton with death or some form of torture growing up?" his mom asks me with a smile and then answers her own question. "Every day. Every day of his life, he was always doing something to drive me to the brink of a meltdown."

"It's true," his dad agrees, coming over in jeans and a hoodie with a football team logo on the front, giving me a quick hug before taking a seat on one of the stools.

I look at Braxton and see the look on his face and can't help but laugh. "Thanks, guys," he mutters, and I laugh harder.

His mom comes around to me, looking stylish in a pair of jeans and a white button-down shirt. She grabs my upper arms, holding my gaze. "The point is we know how frustrating our son can be. So there is nothing you don't feel right now that we haven't felt before."

"Again, thanks." Braxton sighs.

"What? We all need to stick together." His mom smiles.

"You mean you guys all want her to join in on ganging up on me."

"The more, the merrier," his dad says, lifting a cup of coffee my way and making me smile.

"Well, I'm glad to know I'm not alone, and

I'm really sorry about my appearance." I glare at Braxton quickly. "I was trying to go to my place to find something to wear, so I could avoid meeting you looking like this."

His mom squeezes my arms. "Braxton was just explaining to us that your apartment was broken into and that most of your things were destroyed. I'm sorry, and if it helps, I think you look adorable."

"Thanks." I shift on my feet, no longer worried about meeting his parents but wondering if it's too soon to say I might just love them.

"I can go out and pick you something up," she offers, letting my hand go. "At least something for you to wear, so you don't feel uncomfortable, and then we can go sort out your place, make a list of what else you need, and go pick it up."

"You just want a reason to go shop," Bret chimes in. "Not that you ever need a reason to shop." Alisha smiles at her husband then walks over to where he's sitting and kisses his cheek.

"Do you mind if my mom goes to pick you some stuff up?" Braxton asks me softly, and I notice then he's holding a cup of tea out to me.

"Are you sure you wouldn't mind?" I ask Alisha.

"I'm afraid my husband is right. I don't need much of a reason to go shopping," she says, taking her phone out of her bag and bringing it to me. "Just write out what you need and your sizes, and I'll have Bret drive me down the road to Target."

I take her phone and quickly text out the basics.

When I'm done, I start to hand her the phone back then shake my head. "I'm so sorry. I don't have any money on me, and I don't know where my purse is." I start to delete the text, but Braxton takes the phone from me before I can then starts to type.

"Here, Mom." He hands the phone to her then takes a plain black card out of his wallet, handing it to her. "Get what's on the list and anything else you think she might need."

"You got it." She seems all too happy about spending his money, but I don't like the feeling in the pit of my stomach.

"Please don't," I say softly, and she looks at me. "I just need a couple things to hold me over. I'll get the rest this afternoon after I track down my purse."

She looks between me and Braxton, and I don't know her well enough to know what she's thinking, but after a moment, she locks eyes with me and nods before turning on her heel and grabbing her bag. "Let's go, old man."

"We'll be back." Bret stands, grabbing his keys off the counter, not looking as happy as his wife is about a trip to the store.

Once they're gone, I take a seat at the island with my tea, and Braxton goes to the door, locking it. When he comes back to me, he wraps his arms around me and nuzzles the side of my neck, and then he whispers in my ear, making me shiver. "Just a guess, but I don't think my parents hate you."

"Don't be smug." I tip my head to the side as he

kisses down my throat then whimper as he cups one of my breasts and slides his hand down my stomach to cup me between my legs. "Braxton."

"Open your legs for me, Dakota."

Panting, I do as he asked, and he moves his hand under the waistband of his boxers and his fingers slip between my folds. The second he circles my clit, my head drops back and I moan.

"Do you know how soft you are here?" He thrusts two fingers inside me. "How tight and wet you are? How much I love the little sounds you make and the way your pussy flutters when you're about to come?" His breath brushes my ear as my core starts to tighten around his fingers. "Let go."

"Oh, God." My legs start to shake, and stars start to dot my vision as my fingers clench the edge of the chair, but as the orgasm starts to build, he removes his hand. "Don't stop."

I hear him chuckle as he spins the stool around, and then the next thing I know, his boxers I'm wearing are gone, he's on his knees, and his face is between my legs. I rest one foot on his shoulder and the other to the edge of the counter, and he groans as he devours me, his fingers delving into me as he licks and sucks my clit.

The orgasm that had been building comes back with gusto and my head falls back to my shoulders as I tumble over the edge. My heart pounding and my breath coming in short pants, I lift my head and run my fingers through his hair, focusing on his gorgeous face as he stands and looms over me. His gaze stays locked on mine, and I watch a million questions and emotions flash through his eyes.

"What?" I ask quietly, cupping his jaw.

"I'll tell you when the time's right." He takes my arms and lifts them to wrap around his shoulders then grabs me by the back of my knees, lifting me up. I wrap my legs around his waist and hold him while he carries me to the couch, sitting down with me straddling his lap.

I lift my arms as he takes off my shirt, then my hips, and then I watch him pull himself free from his sweats. He slides his length back and forth through my folds as my nails dig into his shoulder. "Take me slow," he orders as he holds himself steady, and I lower myself, biting my lip against the exquisite feel of him filling me. "Yes," he hisses, grabbing my ass with one hand and the back of my neck with the other.

I rise and fall slowly, enjoying the connection, the look on his face, the feel of his skin against mine. He pulls me forward, and I open my mouth over his as he urges me to ride faster while he takes control of the kiss. I let him lead the way, knowing he's never failed to take me somewhere beautiful.

He pulls his mouth from mine, and I rest my forehead against his as he grabs my ass with both hands and his hips start to rise and fall to meet mine, the two of us working in sync, in search of pleasure. When my inner walls begin to pulse, he groans then urges me to go faster, to ride him harder. I try, but my own orgasm makes my body give out, and then he flips me to my back and lifts my legs to his shoulders, fucking me hard. So hard there is a pinch of pain that only seems to intensify the pleasure that is coursing through my body.

His hips jerk then his strokes slow and he lowers my legs from where they are resting. He kisses me once more, this time gentle and sweet, like he's reminding me that no matter how hard he takes me, he can still be soft and tender. When the kiss slows, he picks me up without breaking our connection and carries me into his room. He puts one knee then the other onto the bed then lowers me down, and I whimper at the loss of him.

"I'll be right back." He kisses my forehead, nose, and lips then leans back and tosses the sheet over me and goes into the bathroom. I hear the water turn on, and a few minutes later, he comes out with a washrag he uses to clean me up before kissing my stomach. When our eyes meet, he pulls the sheet back over me then takes the rag back into the bathroom.

When he comes back out, he's dressed in jeans and a black T-shirt. I sit up holding the sheet to my chest then lean back against the headboard and watch him approach me.

"Can you please go check your car for my bag?"

He puts a fist in the bed and looms over me as he answers with a quiet "No."

"Braxton. I'm happy and relaxed. Don't ruin that by being annoying."

He smiles and ducks his head so his lips brush my ear as he speaks. "Your bag is sitting on the table near the front door. If you hadn't been set on running, you would have noticed it earlier."

"You knew where it was," I accuse, leaning back to meet his gaze.

"I saw it when I locked the door so my parents wouldn't walk in on me fucking you."

Oh my God, I didn't even think about them coming back in after they left. My cheeks get pink and he laughs.

"You're evil."

"Yet, you love me." He smirks, and my heart pounds, because he might just be right.

I might just be in love with him.

Damn

Chapter 14

DAKOTA

"THEY LOOK HAPPY."

At that comment from Braxton, I look a little more closely at the still wet photo of my parents I'm holding. My dad's wearing a jean jacket with my mom on his back, looking over the top of his head and smiling. Both of them look young; the picture was probably taken when they first got together or not long after.

"They were." I lick my lips as his arms wrap around me. "They loved each other. They were inseparable." Tears make the back of my throat uncomfortably tight. "It's hard to remember that they were happy, that we were all happy. It's like all the painful parts of my childhood have overshadowed the good times we had before things changed."

"I think that's normal, baby. It's always difficult for

people to remember the good times, especially if those times are connected to something or someone who hurt them." He turns me to face him then looks around my apartment before lowering his voice. "Jamie is going to be here soon. Why don't you go up to my place to wait for him and I'll take care of things here?"

"I don't think it will take me much longer to get things picked up." It's a lie. I thought I remembered from last night how bad things were, but I was wrong. It's taken me over an hour with help from Braxton and his parents to get all my photos picked up and placed on the counters to dry, but my clothes and other things are still scattered across the apartment and shoved in the sink and the bathtub that are still filled with water.

"Dakota!" Alisha calls, dragging my attention away from her son. "Why don't you let me and Bret gather the stuff we think is salvageable, and then Braxton can have everything else taken care of?"

I look from her to her husband. Since the moment I came out dressed in the clothes they went out to pick up for me, they have been at my side, wanting to pitch in and help in whatever way they can. I start to look around but stop when she takes my hand.

"I know you want to be here, but—" She pauses, glancing around still looking as worried as she did the moment she walked in here earlier. "—I don't think you should be."

I drag in a breath then nod, knowing she's right, and now that I've gotten my photos picked up, the rest doesn't really matter anyway. "Okay." I give her a hug. "Thank you."

"You're welcome," she says quietly then lets me go and looks at her son. "Take her upstairs."

Without another word, Braxton leads me from my apartment to the elevator, and moments later holding my fish, we are stepping into his place. I place the small bowl on the counter in the kitchen then go to the couch and fall to my back. I shouldn't be tired, but I feel exhausted. I need a vacation, a long one.

"Do you want some tea?" he asks, and I make an affirmative grunting noise.

"I'm taking that as a yes." He laughs from the kitchen.

I peek one eye open when Braxton comes over and sits on the coffee table then sit up when he holds a cup out toward me. "Thanks." I take the mug from him and check him out as he leans forward, resting his elbows on his knees, a move that causes the black T-shirt he's wearing to stretch across his shoulders, and the muscles in his arms to flex. "I like you in regular-people clothes."

"Regular-people clothes?"

"I'm used to seeing you in suits or dress clothes, but you look good wearing jeans and T-shirts."

"Hmm."

I take a sip of tea then ask, "Would you think less of me if I used the fact that I'm sleeping with you to get a vacation?"

"What?" He laughs.

"Well, I need a vacation, but I just started working

for IMG, so I don't think it will get approved. But since I'm sleeping with you, do you think you can pull some strings?"

"It depends."

"On what?" I raise a brow.

"Exactly what would you be willing to do in order to get this vacation?"

"I think that question would be considered sexual harassment," I say as he takes the cup from my hand and sets it on the table. Then he crowds my space until I'm lying back on the couch. "What are you doing, Mr. Adams?"

He opens his mouth to reply, but an annoying buzzing sound breaks into the moment and he groans, resting his forehead to mine. "That's probably your brother."

"I want this day to be over already." I sigh, and he laughs, pushing away from me. He goes to the intercom on the wall in the kitchen, and I listen to him tell security that Jamie is allowed up. What feels like seconds later, the elevator doors open and my brother steps out. I don't even bother getting up from the couch to greet him. I wait for him to come to me, and when he does, he frowns down at me.

"What's wrong?"

"We need to have a conversation," Braxton tells him, bringing two beers over and handing one to Jamie.

"Are you two having a baby?"

I glance at Braxton, wondering what the look on his face means, and quickly say, "I'm not pregnant."

Jamie visibly relaxes, but I'm too chicken to look at Braxton again. I'm on birth control, not that Braxton and I have ever once discussed that or children. I don't even know if he wants a family someday. I hope he does, because that is something I for sure want, and I know if he doesn't, this will never work. "Can you sit down?" I pat the couch next to me, and after Jamie sits, I take his hand.

"What the fuck is going on? You two are freaking me out."

"Last night, someone broke into my place and trashed it," I tell him, expecting him to react, but he just stares at me, unblinking. "I wasn't home. Braxton and I were at his cabin."

"I have people looking into things," Braxton cuts in, sitting on the couch on the opposite side of me. "The cops are involved and up to date on what's happened."

"Do you have any idea who did it?" Jamie finally speaks, and I look at Braxton. He's been on the phone all day off and on with the cops and the people he hired, but has been keeping things to himself, so I don't really know what's going on.

"We don't." Braxton rests his hand on my thigh. "We're still waiting for them to look at the footage from the cameras in the building, and the police are running the prints they picked up off the package, but it might be a few days before we hear anything from that."

Jamie mumbles something I can't understand as he scrubs his hands down his face, and then he runs his hands through his hair. "So, until then?"

"We just have to wait." I shrug. "I know it sucks, but there is nothing else we can do right now."

"Are you going to stay here with him or do you want to come stay with me at my apartment?" he asks, and Braxton stiffens, his hold on my thigh becoming almost painful.

"I'm going to stay here." I lower my voice when I have his attention then continue, "Please don't be mad." I don't want to upset him or make him feel that I'm choosing Braxton over him, but I feel safe here. Even with everything going on, I'm not afraid, and I know that's because of the man at my side.

"I'm not upset. I get it. Besides, I think you're safer here anyway." He leans back to rest his ankle on his knee. "I'm gonna tell the guys what's going on, and they might want to come check on you."

"They're welcome here anytime," Braxton says, and I cover his hand with mine, giving it a squeeze, hoping he understands how much that tiny gesture means to me. "What are you doing tonight?"

"Nothing, what's up?" Jamie asks.

"My parents are here, and we're planning on going out to dinner. You can join us if you like."

"Please join us." I hold my hands in the prayer position.

Jamie smiles at me. "Yeah, all right," he agrees, and I lean over and hug him. When I let him go, he stands, locking eyes with Braxton. "Since I'm here, why don't you give me a tour of your pad?"

Without a word, Braxton kisses the side of my head and gets up.

I look between the two of them and fight the urge to roll my eyes. "You two do know I'm not an idiot, right? I know you're going to go talk about me." I wave them away. "Go on. Go make each other feel better."

Both men laugh as they walk off, and I smile to myself.

I pick my cup of tea back up and take a sip, relieved that's done and wondering what's next and what will happen when this is over. Until yesterday, I didn't know Braxton had a valid reason for his over-the-top behavior. I didn't know there was a viable threat against me, a threat that was a catalyst for his overprotectiveness. I just wonder how much he will change when this situation is taken care of. A small part of me hopes he doesn't change too much. I like that he's protective and possessive. I like that he cares enough about me to worry. Then again, maybe I'm just as crazy as he is.

Shutting the door on the dishwasher a little later, I hear the front door open right before Alisha and Bret appear carrying large black garbage bags that are leaving a trail of water across the floor.

"Girl, if I find out who did that to your apartment, I'm going to shoot them," Bret grumbles in my direction before taking the bag from Alisha and carrying it to where I know the laundry room is. I watch him go, wondering if I messed up. Maybe I should have stayed to clean up and not allowed them to help.

"We saved a lot of your clothes. They just need to be washed," Alisha tells me as I grab a towel to clean up the floor. "And I put all your underthings in a separate bag, since I didn't know if you would want to keep them."

I meet her concerned gaze. "I really appreciate you doing that."

"You're welcome." She looks to where her husband just disappeared then whispers, "Bret isn't mad at you; he's just really worried about this situation. We both are."

I chew the inside of my cheek. I don't want Braxton's parents worrying because my presence could put their son in danger. Maybe I should go stay with Jamie for a few days, or just until things get cleared up.

"I think I'm going to go stay with my brother," I say, and she blinks at me. "He's here now." I look around then shake my head. "He and Braxton are talking somewhere. He's going to come to dinner with us tonight, but I'll go home with him after."

"Dakota, I don't—"

"Mom," Braxton interrupts whatever she's about to say, and we both turn our attention his way.

"Hey, honey." She seems to force a smile at him then looks at Jamie. "You must be Dakota's brother."

"That's me." Jamie, ever the charmer, comes forward to shake her hand and kisses her cheek. "It's nice to meet you."

"You too." She motions to Bret when he appears around the corner, and I watch the three of them make introductions.

"Are you okay?" Braxton asks, lacing his fingers through mine, and I lick my lips as I look up at him.

"Yeah."

His brows drag together as his eyes search mine. "What happened?"

"Nothing." My immediate response doesn't seem to do anything but annoy him, judging by the look he gives me.

"Dakota."

"I'm fine." I take my hand from his and turn to rest my palms against his chest. "This is all just a lot."

His expression gentles and he rests his forehead on mine. "Trust me when I tell you it will be okay and that I won't let anything happen to you."

"I do trust you." I realize it's not a lie; I do trust him. I don't know when it happened, but somewhere along the way, he proved that I could. I close my eyes and move my hands up to his shoulders then lift up to touch my mouth to his but stop when his phone rings. "I really hate that thing."

"Me too." He sighs then lets me go to take the call. I go back to wiping up the floor as my brother and Braxton's parents talk in the living room, and when I'm done, I head to the laundry room. I open one of the bags of wet clothes and start dumping handfuls of them into the washer.

"Hey." I glance over my shoulder at Jamie. "I'm going to head home. I'll meet you guys at the restaurant tonight," he says and I notice that he seems a little on edge.

"Are you sure you don't want to hang out here until then?" I ask, thinking it would be nice to have him here to take some of the pressure off me.

"I have something I need to take care of," he says, coming to give me a hug. "I'll see you tonight."

"See you tonight," I reply, and he disappears. I start the machine, swearing I hear new voices in the living room, so I head that way and come to a stop when I see Samantha and Hanna standing in the middle of the room surrounded by shopping bags.

Samantha is the first to spot me, and when she does, she rushes across the room and wraps me in a hug. "Are you okay?"

"I'm fine," I assure her. "What are you doing here?"

"Hanna called." She lets me go and waves out toward the woman across the room. "She told me what happened then asked if I would help her pick you some stuff up."

I lock eyes with Hanna and smile softly. "Thank you."

"I'm so sorry, Dakota," she says, and I look at the pink, black, white, and classic brown bags littering the floor. "Braxton asked me to pick you some stuff up, and I might have gone a little overboard. But who could blame me? It's not often a woman is allowed to shop without a budget." I hear the smile in her voice, but my eyes lock on the man who did this, the man who is constantly doing things to show me that he wants to take care of me. Maybe he's right, maybe I need to put away my pride and allow him to take care of me. I also need him to understand that I do appreciate everything he's done.

I pull my eyes off his and take Samantha and Hanna's hands. "Thank you both for doing this. I really appreciate it."

"It was fun." Samantha laughs.

"A lot of fun," Hanna agrees. "And really, we were just glad we could help."

"Do you girls mind helping me get all this stuff put away?" Alisha asks, gathering up a handful of bags, and both the girls follow her lead and head toward Braxton's room carrying everything with them.

"Can I talk to you a second?" I ask Braxton, and he pushes off the couch and follows me around the corner, back into the laundry room. I stand back, holding the door open, and after he enters, I shut it.

He walks to the opposite side of the room from me and crosses his arms over his chest. "Don't be pissed I bought you stuff."

"Shut up." I throw myself against him and press up on my tiptoes so I can cover his mouth with mine. I kiss him with everything I have and hope he understands just how much what he did means. As usual, he takes over. He lifts me off the ground, turning to press my back to the wall and thrusting his tongue into my mouth as I cling to him.

"You're welcome." He rips his mouth from mine, and I smile. "Clean out a couple drawers and move whatever you need to in order to make room for your shit in my closet and bathroom."

"Braxton—"

"Don't argue with me, Dakota," he cuts me off before I can tell him that's not necessary and that I will be going back to my place as soon as I can. "Just do it."

"All right," I give in when I see how determined he is. "Besides, I don't think anyone needs a drawer for ties that all look the same."

"You don't like my ties?"

"I didn't say that. I'm just saying they all look the same, black, gray, or navy. I think you should add some color. How do you feel about pink?"

"No."

"No, you don't like pink, or no, you won't wear a pink tie?"

"Both," he says, and I grin. "What's that grin about?"

"Nothing." I kiss him then attempt to wiggle out of his hold. I let my head fall back in exasperation when he doesn't let me go. "I have stuff to do," I remind him.

He studies me for a moment then drops me to my feet but doesn't release me completely. "I'll be in the living room if there is anything you want me to help you try on."

I laugh and pat his chest. "I'll make sure to let you know if I need your help."

I catch him adjusting himself as I leave, and then I head into his room and make room for myself in his closet, trying to figure out how I'm going to tell him that I won't be staying with him.

Dressed and ready for dinner in the body-hugging, long-sleeved black dress Hanna and Samantha picked up for me, I place my purse on the bed so I can pack it with the stuff I'll need tonight and tomorrow morning. I haven't had the courage to tell Braxton I will be going home with Jamie, and I didn't tell Jamie, since he left after letting me know he'd meet us at the restaurant. I'm hoping that if I spring the news on him at the last minute with my brother present, he will be more accepting of the change of plans.

I put my panties, a bra, and clothes for tomorrow in my bag then go to the bathroom to grab most of the toiletries Alisha put away earlier. With my hands full, I walk to the bed and drop the items. It's going to take some work to make everything fit. As I'm attempting to play Tetris with the items, the bedroom door opens and I toss the end of the blanket over my purse.

"Hey," I squeak, taking a seat and trying to look as casual as possible as Braxton closes the door. The black dress shirt and gray slacks look as good on him as his jeans and T-shirt from earlier did. "I'm just about ready."

"What are you doing?" He eyes me then the bed, and I lean back to hide the lump behind me and lift my leg to touch my ankle.

"Just stretching." I drop my foot and raise my arms over my head. "I always stretch when I know I'm going to be wearing heels." Wow, I sound like an idiot.

"And what is it you are trying to hide behind your

back?" He takes a step toward me, and I lean back farther.

"I'm not hiding anything. Why would I be hiding something?" I ask, and just then my brand new bottle of conditioner rolls onto the floor, stopping at his feet. He bends and picks it up then flips it over in his hand to read the label. "Oh… I wonder how that got in here." I reach up to take it from him, but when I do, he tosses the blanket back, exposing my bag.

"Are you planning on going somewhere?"

"Yes, we're going to dinner, remember?" I cringe as he pulls the things from my bag. "You never know when you might need a change of clothes." I bite my nail, and he rolls his eyes at me while grabbing hold of my wrist.

"You're a horrible liar."

"You would know, since you're the best," I snip, but he doesn't react to my comment.

"My mother just mentioned to me that you might have misinterpreted what she said to you earlier."

"What she said earlier?" I attempt to play stupid, and he glares at me.

"About her and dad being worried, Dakota."

"Oh that," I say as I start repacking my bag. "They have a reason to be worried, and there are no hard feelings on my part." I frown as he takes the things out of my purse, but I otherwise don't react. I just put them back in without looking at him while saying, "After thinking about it, I know me being here might put you in danger, and I don't want that, so I'm going to go home with Jamie after dinner."

"So you're going to go stay with Jamie and put him in danger?" He picks up my purse and tosses it toward the headboard.

I look up at him as my nose scrunches in annoyance, because I didn't think about that. "I'm going to stay in a hotel."

"You're going to stay in a hotel."

"That's what I just said."

"So you're going to tell Jamie and my parents, who are all worried about your safety, that you're going to get a hotel, alone."

"Your parents will be happy you're not in danger, and Jamie will be okay once I explain to him why I'm going to stay in a hotel."

"My parents will be happy when they know I'm not in danger?"

Even though his tone and the look he gives me are filled with warning, I still say, "Yeah."

He eyes me for a moment then shakes his head. "I don't have time to deal with this right now. We have a reservation to get to."

"What?" I stand up and follow him through the bathroom and into the closet. When he doesn't respond, I ask, "What does that mean?"

He turns to face me as he slips on a suit jacket that matches his slacks. "It means I'm not going to waste my breath arguing with you, since one way or another, you will be coming home with me tonight."

"So you don't care that your parents are worried

about you?" I cross my arms over my chest and block the doorway when he takes a step toward me.

"They aren't worried about me. They're worried about you."

My brows drag together. "They don't know me enough to care about what happens to me."

"They know I'm falling in love with you, Dakota. They know that if something happens to you, it would kill me. So yes, they're worried about me, but it's because they are worried about something happening to you," he growls, and then he stomps to me, grabbing my hand and glaring down at me. "Now we need to get to dinner."

I stumble, the words "I'm falling in love with you" dancing through my head and making me dizzy as he practically drags me from the room.

"Is everything okay?" his mom asks, standing from the couch and glancing worriedly between us when we reach the living room.

I don't know about the man still holding my hand, but I'm so *not* okay right now. I feel lightheaded, nauseous, and if I don't take a breath soon, I might pass out from lack of oxygen.

"We're fine," Braxton states, and I catch his parents' look at each other before he pulls me with him to the elevator. Once we are all inside and the doors are closed, the silence becomes uncomfortable, and I shift in my heels then look up at Braxton, watching the muscles in his jaw twitch.

"You look nice, Dakota," Alisha says, breaking

into the silence, and I pull my attention off her son's ticking jaw to look at her, noticing she changed into a simple cream dress with a colorful shawl around her shoulders. Bret is now wearing a dress shirt and slacks. The two of them look like the proud parents of a well-established businessman.

"Thanks, you both look nice too." I force a smile, and Braxton squeezes my fingers still laced between his.

When we reach the parking garage, we all go to his Benz and Braxton opens my door for me to get in. I hesitate and look up at him. There are hundreds of things I want to tell him, but when he drops his eyes to me, everything gets stuck on the tip of my tongue. With a quiet sigh, I climb into my seat and he slams my door closed.

I watch him walk around the hood, then a moment later, he slides in behind the wheel, giving me a look that has me quickly putting on my seat belt. He starts the engine, and I reach over the console between us to rest my hand on his thigh, and when he covers my hand with his, I let out the breath I've been holding, wishing I was brave enough to tell him that I love him too.

Chapter 15

DAKOTA

WITH BRAXTON AND his parents distracted, I look under the edge of the table and tap Braxton's watch to see the time then shake my head. Jamie is now almost an hour late.

"He's probably caught in traffic." Braxton's words startle me, and I glance at him as he gives my thigh a gentle squeeze.

"You're probably right." Worry and frustration fill the pit of my stomach. I wish I could say it's not like Jamie to run late, but I don't think he's ever shown up for anything on time. I just thought he knew I needed him tonight.

"He'll be here."

"He better be," I mutter back as I pick up my glass of wine. I swallow a huge gulp then look at Braxton's parents, who are watching me, and set down my glass. All I need is for them to think I have an issue with alcohol on top of being a danger to their son's life.

"Dakota," Bret calls, and I focus on him, my muscles getting tight when I see the look of concern in his eyes. "I think I need to apologize." He clears his throat, and Alisha covers his hand with hers on the table. "I was upset earlier after seeing what was done to your apartment, but I wasn't upset with you."

"Neither of us are upset with you," Alisha chimes in with a soft smile, and Braxton's hand smooths up and down my thigh.

"We know what's happening isn't your fault, and both of us agree that the safest place for you to be is with our son." He smiles a smile that looks like one of his son's. "That's unless you say you want to come home with us when we leave."

I laugh, relieved they don't hate me. "I do need a vacation. I might just take you up on that."

"You're welcome anytime." Alisha says, and Bret nods his agreement as Braxton's cell phone begins to ring. I glare at his phone when he pulls it from his pocket and then seethe at him.

"Seriously, I really hate that stupid thing," I tell him as he looks at his phone, seeming confused.

"Sorry." He kisses my cheek. "I'll be right back." He stands, placing his napkin on the table before walking away. I turn to look over my shoulder and watch him disappear through the crowded restaurant, putting his phone to his ear when he reaches the door.

"Well." I pick my glass of wine back up as I look between Bret and Alisha. "If you don't hear from your son, it's because I've either killed him or tossed his cell into the trash." They both laugh as I take another gulp of wine, thinking they really shouldn't be so stingy with their servings, especially since I know this wine didn't cost thousands of dollars.

"You're good for him," Bret states softly as I set my now empty glass down and look at him. "You aren't afraid to remind him that work isn't the most important thing in his life."

"Yet he still just left the table with his phone," I point out.

Alisha shrugs. "We're hoping that the more you point it out, the more he will see how much his job has taken over his life."

"Don't get your hopes up," I say then jump when a hand lands on my shoulder. I tip my head back and meet Braxton's gaze, and the look in his eyes sends a chill down my spine.

"What happened?" I ask as he takes his seat next to me and adjusts me in my chair so that I'm facing him. "You're scaring me," I admit as he takes my hands.

"That call was from your brother."

"Jamie," I whisper, and he nods.

"He was arrested tonight."

My stomach drops, and I turn my hands over so I'm gripping his. "Arrested?"

"Freddie got drunk and started rambling about you and me to Lozz. At first, he didn't think much of it, but then Lozz spoke to Jamie, and your brother told him about your place being trashed and what's been happening. Lozz put two and two together, since he knew Freddie didn't go home with them Friday. Jamie went over to talk to him, and Freddie was still drunk and admitted what he did."

"What?" I whisper, sure I heard him wrong.

"Things became violent, they fought, and Freddie is in the hospital. Jamie is at the station."

My stomach churns. "I think I'm going to be sick." I pull my hand from his to cover my mouth. I haven't known Freddie as long as I've known Jinx and Lozz, but he's still someone I trust—one of the few people I really trust.

"I called my lawyer. He's going down to the station to bail Jamie out, but he did a number on Freddie, so we need to be prepared for what might happen."

I close my eyes and drop my chin to my chest. Jamie has always had a temper, and when he loses control of it, he becomes irrational and can't restrain himself. I can only imagine what he did to Freddie when he found out he was the one behind what's been going on, especially when he considered him a close friend.

"I just can't believe this." I want to ask why, want to understand, but right now isn't the time for me to ask questions. Right now, I need to get myself together and make sure I'm ready to help Jamie, because it seems like he's going to need me. "How long do you think it will be before your lawyer gets him out?"

He checks his watch. "My guess—an hour, maybe

two.”

“I want to be there,” I say, and he shakes his head. “Don’t tell me no, Braxton.”

“I don’t want you at the police station. I’ll have my lawyer bring him to my place. He can stay with us there while we wait to find out how Freddie is.”

Freddie. I don’t want to be worried about him, but I am, and I’m sure Jamie is too. “Exactly how bad is he?”

“Jamie didn’t know. He just said he was bad and unconscious when the EMTs took him away. I’ll make a couple calls and find out when we get home.”

“Okay,” I say then look at Alisha and Bret. “I’m sorry about this.”

“Don’t apologize,” Alisha says softly.

“I’m going to pay the bill,” Bret adds then looks at Braxton. “Why don’t you and your mom get Dakota to the car?”

Without a word, he stands, bringing me up with him, then he leads his mom and me through the restaurant. When we get outside, he leaves Alisha and me to wait under the awning near a warming light while he goes to the valet stand. It’s not freezing, but the temperature has dropped enough to make me wish I had my jacket. I wrap my arms around my middle, and a moment later, Braxton comes over and slips off his jacket, wrapping it around my shoulders.

“Thank you.” I lean into him as his arm circles my waist, and then we wait in silence for his car, the knot in my stomach growing by the second. If I had my cell, I could call Lozz or Jinx and ask them what they know, but now all I can do is think of every worst-case scenario.

An hour later, I sit on the couch with a cup of tea in front of me, my leg bouncing up and down as I stare at the elevator. Braxton came out of his office a few minutes ago to let me know Jamie is on the way and that Jinx and Lozz are with him.

Since we got home, he and his dad have been on the phone with his lawyer, another lawyer, the police, and the hospital, trying to find out how Freddie is doing. I don't know how I would deal with this situation without them. Even Alisha has been cool and calm, trying to put me at ease.

"Drink some tea," Alisha urges, picking up my cup and handing it to me as the intercom buzzes.

I take it from her and have a sip, wishing the warmth would wash away the worry as she gets up. I listen to her tell security to allow them up, and when the doors to the elevator slide open a few minutes later, Jamie steps out with Lozz, Jinx, and a man wearing a suit following them. My stomach bottoms out and my hands shake when I see the blood on Jamie's shirt, the cut on his lip, and the black eye he's sporting.

He comes to me and takes a seat on the couch at my side with Lozz and Jinx doing the same, the three of them looking somber as I absently hear Alisha tell the lawyer to follow her to Braxton.

I set my cup down, rest my head on Jamie's chest, and stare at the two men sitting opposite us. I want to say something, but I honestly don't have a clue what I could say that would make any of this better.

I look up when Braxton comes into the room, and his eyes soften on me before he walks the lawyer to the elevator. Once the older man is gone, he comes into the living room and looks at my brother. "Freddie is fine," he says, holding Jamie's eye, and I squeeze my brother's waist. "The doctors said he had alcohol poisoning, which is why he blacked out."

"So I didn't hurt him?" Jamie asks, sounding as relieved as I feel.

"You did, but not as bad as you thought you did. They are keeping him in the hospital overnight, and the cops are going to talk to him in the morning when he's sober. There is a chance he could press charges against you, but he's going to have some questions to answer himself, since the cops were able to match his prints to the ones on the box we intercepted."

"I still can't believe he did this shit." Jinx sighs.

"I wish I could tell you it wasn't him, but I found out a few minutes ago that he's on video in the elevator."

"I don't get why he would do it. He never flirted with me, he didn't even really talk to me."

"I knew he had a thing for you," Lozz admits, running his hand through his long hair. "He just wasn't sure if Jamie would be cool with him asking you out, and he wanted to make sure you were over the Troy shit before he did."

"You never mentioned that to me," Jamie says.

Lozz sighs. "I never thought it was a big deal. I sure

as hell didn't think he'd do the shit he did."

"I don't want to bring this up now, but we need to call Dan. We're down a band member, and we're going to have to find someone to replace Freddie before we go on tour."

"Shit," Jamie groans. "I want to kick his ass all over again."

I sit up to make room for Braxton on the couch next to me, and once he's sitting, I curl into his side, resting my cup on his thigh. "You need to wait to see if Freddie presses charges," Braxton says. "If he does, that might make it a little more difficult for you to leave town. If he doesn't, you can explain what's happening and ask if Dan knows someone who can fill in for Freddie until you can find a replacement."

"I didn't really want to call him tonight anyway," Jamie says, and my eyes soften on my brother's tired face.

"Do you want to stay here?" I ask, and Braxton gives my upper arm a squeeze of approval.

"Nah, I'm going to head home." He sits up, patting my leg, and then he eyes Braxton. "Thanks for everything you did tonight, man. I really appreciate it."

"Anytime," Braxton replies quietly, and my throat gets tight with emotion. Somewhere along the way, he and Jamie have formed a bond that is all their own, and that is something I didn't know would be so important to me.

Jamie stands, and Jinx along with Lozz get up as I

push off the couch, pulling Braxton up with me. "How are you guys going to get home?" I ask them when we reach the elevator.

"Don't worry about us. We'll grab a cab when we get downstairs," Lozz tells me, giving me a hug. I hug Jinx next then go to my brother when he opens his arms.

"I'm really glad you're okay." I circle his waist and squeeze as he kisses the top of my head before he releases me.

"Stan will call you in the morning after Freddie speaks with the police. We'll regroup after that," Braxton says.

Jamie takes his hand and orders, "Take care of my sister," patting his shoulder before letting him go.

I watch the three of them get on the elevator then wave as the doors close. Once they're gone, I turn and look up at Braxton, placing my hands on his chest as his settle on my hips. "I changed my mind."

"About what?" he prompts.

"My willingness to do whatever you want in order to get that vacation I mentioned earlier."

He grins then touches his mouth to mine. "I'll keep that in mind."

"I'm ordering Chinese," Alisha says, coming into the room, and I turn to watch her look around. "Oh, your brother and his friends already left." She meets my gaze. "Do you two want something to eat?"

"Please." I rest my hand on my stomach. Now that the drama is over, I'm starving.

"Give me your order." She smiles, and I tell her what I want, and Braxton gives her his order. "It will probably be a while before it gets here, and your dad is taking a nap. He's had a day." She laughs as she walks off, and I couldn't agree more with Bret. It's been a day that's felt like a year. I'm just glad it's over.

I WAKE WHEN Braxton's phone rings, and for the first time ever, I'm not upset, because I can hear the person on the other end of the line explain that Freddie isn't pressing charges against Jamie and that he admitted to what he did to me. When he hangs up the call, I listen to his phone hit the bedside table then cuddle closer to him as he pulls me up so my head is resting against his pec.

"Are you awake?" he asks with his breath brushing my forehead as his fingers skim down my spine.

"Yeah."

"Freddie isn't pressing charges," he tells me—something I already heard.

"Jamie will be happy."

"He's been arrested for what he did to you."

"Good," I mumble, and silence settles between us. I close my eyes and try to sleep, but his statement from yesterday keeps replaying in my mind. "Can I ask you a question?"

"Ask away." His hand moves to my hip to squeeze.

I tip my head back toward him and find his eyes closed. "Do you want kids?"

At my question, his eyes open to meet mine then he rolls me to my back and cups my cheek. "Yes, I want kids."

"How do you feel about adopting?" I ask, holding my breath as his eyes search mine.

"Is that something you want?"

"Yes," I admit quietly. "I want kids of my own, but I also want to adopt. I've always wanted a big family with lots of kids running around."

His eyes soften and he rests his forehead to mine. "I like that idea."

"Can I ask you another question?"

"Yeah." He doesn't move away, so I take a breath to work up the courage to ask what I need to ask.

"Why do you think you're falling in love with me?"

"I don't think I'm falling in love with you." His eyes stay locked with mine as his thumb glides over my jaw. "I *am* in love with you."

"How do you know?"

"How do you know you need to breathe?" he asks in return, and tears start to fill my eyes. "Loving you isn't something I think about. It's something that has happened without me thinking about it and is as natural to me as taking my next breath."

I lift my hand and rest it against his scruffy cheek as tears slide into my hair. "I love you too." The words are harsh as I lean up and press my lips to his. He kisses me back, and I smile against his lips then let my head fall back against the pillow. "How did this happen?"

"Determination." He rolls to his back with me in his arms, and I straddle his waist then look down into his eyes, knowing he's right.

The only explanation for everything that happened between us since the moment we met is his determination to get his way.

I'm just glad that Mr. Wrong ended up being Mr. Right.

Epilogue

Two months later . . .

$\mathcal{I}$ WALK INTO the kitchen glancing along the counters for my cell then go to my office and look under the stack of papers there then into the living room where Dakota is sitting on the couch reading to look around. It's been two months since we found out Freddie was responsible for everything that happened to her. Since then he sat Jamie down and explained that he hoped she would find out about the threat, tell her brother and then step in to save the day. He didn't know about me, but knew his plan wouldn't work when he saw her and I together. That's when he got drunk, stole the watch she had given to Jamie and broke into her place trashing it in a rage. His hope in admitting the truth was that he would be able to go on tour with Jamie and the rest of the guys, but all that happened was Dakota got closure. The guys left him behind, the trust they had built demolished by his actions and now Jamie is on tour with a song playing at number one on every single radio station in the country and in some parts of the world. Dakota has also won over Kathy, or I should say Hanna introduced her family to her new man and Kathy let go of the hope that Hanna and I would end up together. But that doesn't mean that myself or Chris has stopped trying to move Dakota, not that it's worked.

"Can I help you?" Dakota asking that question pulls me from my thoughts and I focus on her, feeling my chest warm. As fucked up as what Freddie did is, I still understand why he would go to such extreme lengths to get her attention. Why he would do something fucked up in the attempt to make her his.

"Have you seen my cell?" I ask narrowing my eyes on her, because my phone seems to disappear a lot when we are home alone together, and then reappear in the oddest places. And I do consider this our home even if she still has her place downstairs. Since I told her I love her we haven't spent a night apart unless I have to be out of town and even then she still stays here.

"Your cell?" She glances around then looks at her book muttering. "I haven't seen it."

"Dakota," I wrap my hands around my hips. "I'm expecting an important call."

She slowly lifts her eyes to meet mine. "Then Braxton you should really be more responsible with your stuff. Plus it's Sunday, no one works on Sunday." Fuck I love her. I had no idea I was capable of loving someone the way I love her. I eye her for a moment then say screw it, work can wait. I go to her and pull the book from her hand then toss it across the room. "Hey, I was reading that."

"To bad, if I can't work you're going to entertain me." I scoop her up and with her laughter ringing through the apartment I carry her to my bed where I spend the rest of the day making love to the woman who changed everything for me.

Eight months later . . .

I SHUT OFF the water and get out of the shower to dry off then tie my towel around my waist. I head into the closet to get dressed, and as I usually do, I place my suit on the chair along with my dress shirt then go to my new tie rack, finding it empty. I frown then go to the drawer my ties used to be in, but it's full of delicate lace.

After searching the closet and coming up empty-handed, I head into the bedroom and blink at the sight that greets me. Dakota is lounging in the middle of the bed, wearing nothing but the engagement ring I put on her finger a month ago and a hot-pink tie, the length resting between her breasts and the end covering what

I know is heaven.

"Are you looking for something, Mr. Adams?"

I smirk and walk across the room, letting the towel drop away and watching her pupils dilate. You'd think that after almost a year with her, things between us would cool down, but so far, they haven't. I'm just as crazy about her now as I was the first moment we met, maybe even crazier.

I crawl up the bed and grab her ankles, pulling them apart before settling between her legs.

"I found it." I drop my mouth to hers and kiss her, then I make love to my fiancée and when I get dressed for work an hour later, I put on that pink tie with a grin on my face.

ACKNOWLEDGMENTS

First I have to give thanks to God, because without him none of this would be possible. Second I want to thank my husband. I love you now and always—thank you for believing in me even when I don't always believe in myself. To my beautiful son, you bringing such joy into my life, and I'm so honored to be your mom.

To every blog and reader, thank you for taking the time to read and share my books. There would never be enough ink in the world to acknowledge you all, but I will forever be grateful to each and every one of you.

I started this writing journey after I fell in love with reading, like thousands of authors before me. I wanted to give people a place to escape where the stories were funny, sweet, and hot and left you feeling good. I have loved sharing my stories with you all, loved that I have helped people escape the real world, even for a moment.

I started writing for me and will continue writing for you. XOXO Aurora